Won't You Be My Master?

Jacqueline Grey

Print ISBN: 978-1-7331722-1-9

Edited by Jenni Lea

Proofing by Jennifer Smith

Cover Illustrations by Xier

Cover Design by Kanaxa

Formatting by Leslie Copeland

First Edition 2022

www.jacquelinegrey.com

About Won't You Be My Master?

What do you do when you find a naked pup in a box? Take him home, of course.

Harold had never heard of pup play before he met Taylor, but he's happy to try new things if it will keep this captivating young man by his side a little longer.

Taylor had never considered belonging to a Master, but Harold makes pup play feel like a natural part of their everyday life.

Both will never look at a box the same way again.

- Harold is lonely and needs a dog
- Taylor is a pup without a Master
- We communicate through banter
- Human dogs have more fun
- Pup play
- Age gap

Chapter One

Harold liked to think of himself as a pretty laid-back person, but today it felt like the universe was conspiring against him. Granted, there was something about airports that would try anyone's patience, but boarding a plane nine hours after he'd been scheduled to fly home seemed like overkill.

He'd love to know what he'd done wrong. He'd make the appropriate recompense, send up as many prayers as required—at this point he'd do anything as long as he made it home safely and before the turn of the next century.

He stowed his carry-on in the overhead compartment and let out a sigh as he dropped into his narrow seat. He'd made it. He was on the plane. Now if only the muscles in his neck and shoulders would relax.

They refused.

"Are you afraid of flying?"

Harold looked over at the person settling in beside him and almost choked on his own breath. The young man was gorgeous, a perfect mix of boyishly cute and ruggedly handsome. His brown eyes were like chocolate, a cliché of a description but Harold couldn't think of another. They were a comfort akin to the treat, full of warmth and concern. His feathered brown hair swept across his forehead, a few locks falling close to his eyes in careless disarray. And his body... Harold couldn't help but admire the snug T-shirt and jeans that clung in all the right places.

He was also young. Not illegal, but he had to be a decade Harold's junior. Yet as Harold stared, he decided he didn't care one bit. If all of the universe's machinations for today had brought him here to meet this man, he was happy to accept the gift.

"I was afraid of never leaving the tarmac," Harold said. "I'm feeling better now."

The man smiled, hopefully picking up on Harold's attempt at flirting. "Is that so?" Oh yes. He'd definitely picked up on it. "What made you so afraid in the first place?"

"The short version? I was supposed to fly out of here at three today. Actually, at this point it was yesterday."

The man's eyes widened. "That's insane. How?"

"Well, apparently, if an airline overbooks your flight, you can be the lucky winner of the 'we're kicking you off this plane and we'll reschedule you for the one at 9:00 p.m.' lottery even if you reserved your ticket months in advance."

"Oh man. And here I thought the three-hour delay because of the weather was bad enough."

He was right. Harold hadn't been the only one who'd had to deal with delays. His had just been longer. The plane was filled with grumpy passengers who were annoyed and tired, wanting desperately to be home just as much as he was. Their irritated complaints blended together with the hum of the engines as they picked up. "At least we're finally moving," he said.

The crackle of speakers heralded the usual safety demonstration followed by a final pre-takeoff announcement from the pilot. Not long after, they were rolling down the runway. Harold and his seatmate were quiet as the pressure of speed pressed them back into their seats. There was a tilt and then they were climbing. Harold had never been more grateful for g-force.

"My name's Taylor," the young man said when they'd evened out again.

"Harold."

"It's nice to meet you, Harold."

"Same here." And it was. All of Harold's frustration had washed away the moment he'd laid eyes on Taylor. The prospect of chatting him up gave Harold a thrill he hadn't felt in a long time. It wouldn't be anything more than simple flirting. Taylor was clearly out of his league. The only time Harold interacted with men that hot was when he watched porn. Guys like that didn't go for forty-year-old computer nerds who preferred staying home with their dogs to going out.

"What do you do, Harold?" Taylor asked.

"I'm a freelance computer programmer."

"Are you one of those lucky people who get to work from home?"

Harold huffed out a laugh. "It's not always lucky, believe me. What about you?"

"I'm an assistant photographer for a production company. Between the studio and location shoots, it's as far from working from home as I can get."

"Must be nice to get to travel for work, though."

"Oh, it is," Taylor said. "Don't get me wrong. I love my job, but sometimes it's tough when we have a bunch of sessions scheduled close together."

"Are you heading to a shoot or home from one?"

"Home, but I don't get to stay long. We're flying out again on Wednesday for Colorado. Thankfully, I have the weekend off so I can unwind a bit." Taylor stretched his arms and legs forward as much as one could in an airplane. "I've been itching to let loose."

Harold could picture Taylor at a club, dancing under the changing lights, his skin sheened in sweat, body lithe and graceful. The image was enthralling. Harold would love nothing more than to be there with him, moving in counterpoint, their bodies touching in a conversation that could only be found on a dance floor.

That fantasy was a far cry from reality. Harold couldn't remember the last time he'd been to a dance club. When was the last time he'd gone out to have fun? Or flirted with someone? Been turned on by a stranger? Or intoxicated by a kiss? Too long. Way too long if he'd forgotten. Harold's most stimulating relationship right now was with his favorite dildo. What made it even sadder was that it had been true even when he'd been dating his ex, Sean, and they'd been together for three years.

Harold had been looking forward to getting home and unwinding with some quality time with said dildo. Now, with thoughts of Taylor echoing in his head, the promise of familiar pleasures was overshadowed by the reality of his empty apartment and the monotony that was his life.

If only Missy were still here to keep me company.

He'd take this conversation, though. It was real and flattering. The attention fed a part of him that had been neglected, and even though he'd return home alone, the feeling of being attractive to someone was worth it.

Their conversation paused as the seatbelt sign blinked

out and one of their fellow travelers took the opportunity to make his clumsy way past for the bathroom.

After making sure no one else was going to elbow him while stumbling by, Taylor asked, "Where are you traveling from?"

"I was visiting my sister, Madeline."

"I take it you're close?"

Harold nodded.

"I'm an only child," Taylor said. "Am I asking too many questions? I don't usually talk to people on planes."

That was a surprise. What was so interesting about Harold that prompted Taylor to talk to him? "No, it's fine. I don't mind."

"That doesn't mean you're particularly thrilled about it," Taylor pointed out.

"Am I supposed to be thrilled?"

"No." Taylor sighed. "I just don't want to bother you, and some people are too polite to say so."

Was Taylor self-conscious? From where Harold sat, he had no need to feel that way. "I promise you're not bothering me."

"Good."

The pinball of a passenger returned, and Taylor leaned over to keep out of harm's way. Harold caught a whiff of something spicy with a woodsy undertone. Definitely not hotel soap. Perhaps aftershave or cologne? Harold inched closer to inhale more of the delicious scent.

When safety reigned once again, Taylor straightened. The movement startled Harold into sitting up as well. Embarrassed by his actions and the curious look Taylor was giving him, he asked the first thing that came to mind.

"Are you seeing someone?"

With the words free in the universe and unable to be retracted, he inwardly flinched. *Why did I ask that?*

Taylor's lips quirked into a knowing smirk, and Harold wanted to dissolve into his seat. It wasn't as if he had a chance with Taylor. Nor did he want one. He wasn't ready for a relationship again.

Yeah, that was a lie.

"My boyfriend and I live together," Taylor said.

Disappointment hit Harold like an unexpected blow to the chest, which was ridiculous since they'd only been casually flirting. He hoped the emotion didn't show on his face when he replied, "That's great."

It wasn't great, and Taylor didn't think Harold believed it either, but the older man didn't know the half of it. The words had slipped out purely out of habit; they weren't true anymore, and the truth was complicated. He and Liam never should have started dating, but it had taken them three months to admit that. Then, when they had, they'd been stuck with a lease neither of them could afford by themselves, nor could they afford to break it. It had left them in a weird, undefined limbo of a relationship.

Thankfully, there were only six weeks left to go before their lease was up. Taylor had marked the date in bright yellow on his Google calendar like a light at the end of a very long tunnel.

He didn't want to dump all that on Harold, though. Harold seemed like a nice guy and didn't need any of Taylor's baggage. No, he deserved worship and someone to call him Daddy. Or, better yet, Master.

Did the man even know how hot he was? Probably not.

His attempts at flirting had lacked self-assurance and the expectation of results. Taylor had been subjected to that sort of arrogance enough to recognize when it wasn't there.

That obliviousness was part of Harold's charm, on top of the fact that he was Taylor's personal wet dream. Okay, he didn't have the solid muscle of someone who lived at the gym, but he was more fit than Taylor would expect from someone who spent all their time in front of a computer. He obviously took care of himself and would be perfectly capable of holding Taylor down while he pleaded and squirmed. Taylor would helplessly clutch those broad shoulders and beg until he was allowed to come.

Not the time to get an erection, Taylor thought. He shifted in his seat, trying to make the movement subtle.

Harold was hairy too. Not overly, but enough that Taylor could imagine the curls that would undoubtedly be on his chest. He'd feel them brush against his skin if Harold fucked him.

Seriously, brain. Now is not the time nor the place!

Best of all was Harold's beard. It was thick and luxurious, and Taylor wanted to rub his face all over it.

Oh yes, Taylor would happily call Harold Master. In fact, he'd beg to. He wanted to beg right now. Too bad Taylor wasn't in a position to make an offer. Or was he? It wasn't like he and Liam were still dating. Technically, he was free to pursue anyone he wanted. It was just weird when his ex was still living with him.

"Are you seeing anyone?" Taylor asked.

Harold shook his head. "Not for a while."

Taylor's heart rejoiced at the knowledge. The temptation to ask for a date thrummed through him like a bowstring, but he'd told Harold he was still with Liam. What would Harold think if he backtracked now?

"What happened?" Taylor asked instead.

"We didn't work."

"I'm sorry."

Harold shrugged. "It was for the best. I was more upset about losing Missy than losing him."

"Missy?"

"Our dog. We adopted her not long after we'd moved in together."

"He took the dog?" Taylor asked incredulously. "That's terrible."

"No, he left both me and Missy. She passed away six months ago."

"I'm so sorry." And this time he meant it.

"Thank you. Is it weird? Being more upset about losing a dog than losing my boyfriend?"

"Of course not! Animals are family. Obviously, your boyfriend wasn't."

Harold's lips quirked into a smile.

"How long were you together?" Taylor asked.

"Three years. We moved in after two and that's when we got Missy."

"Do you have pictures?" At Harold's look, he clarified. "Of the dog."

"Oh." Harold took out his phone and started scrolling. It didn't take long for him to find what he was looking for, and in moments Taylor was shown a picture of a golden retriever in mid-run through a backyard on a sunny day.

"She's gorgeous," he said.

"She was." Harold flipped through the album and showed Taylor another picture. This time the dog was jumping to catch a Frisbee. Over the next ten minutes they perused various photos of the canine. She was alone in most of them, but some were with Harold, and occasionally another man appeared. He was handsome with one of those smiles people paid a fortune for. Taylor assumed he was Harold's ex.

It was clear Harold had cared a great deal for Missy. Though his expression was tinged with sadness, he smiled fondly at the pictures.

"How old was she?" Taylor asked.

"She was six when we got her. Sean wanted a puppy, but they get adopted so easily. I wanted to give a home to an animal that had less of a chance of being chosen. When I saw Missy, it was love at first sight."

Could the man be any more of a sweetheart? Taylor wanted to curl up in his lap to be petted like Missy had been three photographs ago.

"Do you have any pets?" Harold asked.

"No. I love animals, but the apartments I've lived in never allowed them." Technically, there had occasionally been a pet in his apartment, but he'd been the pet in question.

Taylor thought back to one photograph of Harold and Missy on the couch, the dog's head in Harold's lap and Harold's fingers running through her fur as he smiled at the camera. What Taylor wouldn't give to take her place in that photo. It had been way too long since he'd had time to indulge in his kink. The weekend couldn't come fast enough.

"Would you consider getting another dog?" he asked.

"I've thought about it," Harold said. "Before Missy I'd only ever taken in strays. They'd always seemed to find me when I was growing up."

"Where'd you grow up?"

"Just outside Duluth. My sister lives in our parents' old house."

"So, your parents are…?" Questions like these were always hard to ask.

"They passed away, yes."

"I'm sorry."

"Thank you."

"Do you have any other siblings?"

"Nope. Just me and my sister. I do have a brother-in-law and a niece, which is why Madeline's decided she's entitled to scold me like a parent from time to time. She thinks I'm lonely."

"All the more reason to get another dog," Taylor teased.

"Yeah," Harold said with a laugh, "but I'll go back to letting them find me."

Taylor's inner pup rolled over and kicked its paws into the air. For a man this kind and thoughtful? "I don't think you'll have a problem with that."

Chapter Two

On the way home from the market Saturday morning, Harold passed a box set out for recycling. One of his neighbors must have gotten a new washing machine or dishwasher because the thing was so huge it covered half the sidewalk. He had to edge around it to get to his apartment building, but it was because of this proximity that he saw the box wasn't empty.

"What the fuck?"

He took a step closer and peered over the edge. No, he wasn't imagining things. There was a naked man in the box. Not completely naked, but with only a G-string on, it was close enough.

Did I just find a dead body? Wait, what idiot would dump a dead body in the middle of a busy sidewalk? Oh my god, please don't be dead, person.

"Hello?" he said tentatively, wondering what he would do if the person really was dead. "Are you alive in there?" *Please, please, please be alive.* He didn't want to have to find out what happened when a civilian found a corpse in reality. He was sure there was more to it than screaming like they showed on TV. *Points to me for not screaming.*

But if the man was alive, how the hell did he end up mostly naked in a box on Harold's sidewalk? This was New York. Tourists were thrilled when they spotted a random half-naked person in Times Square, not fifty blocks away on the Upper West Side.

Harold reined in his panicked thoughts and looked at the body again. It still hadn't moved. *Oh fuck.*

He juggled his bags into one hand and pulled his phone from his pocket. Just as he was about to dial the last number for 911, there was a groan from the cardboard container.

"Oh, thank god!" he exclaimed, shoving his phone back in his pocket. His hands were shaking. They were actually shaking. "Hey, are you all right in there?"

The man shifted, shielding his eyes even though the day was overcast, and peered groggily up at him. Harold didn't see any injuries. *I bet the only "injury" he has is a good old-fashioned hangover.*

Harold held up three fingers. "How many do you see?"

The stranger made the universal tongue movement for a dry mouth before answering. "Three? I think?"

"I'll take it. Can you stand?"

"Maybe." There was a pause. "The room isn't spinning from this angle."

How much had he drunk? "Let's give it a shot then." He held out a hand and the man took it. With Harold's assistance, they got him semi-steadily onto his feet. Now that he was no longer curled up in the box, Harold had an unobstructed view of everything that was on display: a lean frame covered in planes of solid muscle, a hairless body, either by nature or design, and a chiseled face partially obscured by tousled chestnut hair. The man was drool-worthy.

This is the second time in a week that I've met someone who could rival my porn star collection. What are the chances?

That was not a thought he should be having on the sidewalk right outside his apartment building. Which reminded him that they actually were on the sidewalk right outside his apartment building and the man was still only dressed in a G-string. "Shit." He performed an acrobatic scramble to get out of his sweatshirt jacket without putting his shopping bags down. God only knew what was on the sidewalks of New York. He wasn't having it anywhere near his food. "Take this and put it on."

Apparently realizing his own state of undress, the man did. "I think I've lost my phone," he said.

"Not sure where you would have put it," Harold retorted.

"I had a jacket when I went to the party."

"Good to know you don't normally walk around like this."

The man squinted at him. "Why are you giving me attitude?"

Harold wasn't sure. "Sarcasm is my coping mechanism for the surreal."

"I'm as real as they come, baby."

"Are you flirting with me right now?" Harold wasn't sure if he should be frustrated or flattered. He was leaning toward both.

"It's my coping mechanism for morning afters."

Harold laughed.

A woman walking her dog gave them a look as she passed.

"We should get off the sidewalk." Harold gestured ahead of them. "That's my building. How about you come upstairs and borrow a pair of pants?"

"Now who's trying to pick up who?"

"I'm trying to put you into pants, not get you out of them." Although in other circumstances, he would have loved to, given the visual buffet in front of him.

His half-naked temptation sighed. "That's probably a good idea. Help me out of this?"

"How did you manage to get into it in the first place?" Harold mused.

They ended up having to tilt the box while the man used Harold's shoulder to steady himself. He clambered out of the cardboard trap with the coordination of a colt trying to stand for the first time. Success left them only inches apart, the man's arms wrapped around Harold's neck and Harold's hands at his waist. Harold was lost staring into a pair of infinitely deep brown eyes when a sharp whistle broke the spell of the moment.

"Get a room!" someone yelled.

Harold instinctively stepped back. "I'm sorry I—"

"Whoa!" the man called out. Harold grabbed his arm and pulled him forward to keep him from falling, but he pulled too hard, and they collided.

"Sorry!" Harold said again.

"This is too much drama for...what time is it?" the younger man asked. He hadn't moved from Harold's embrace.

"Probably around ten."

"Definitely too much drama for this early on a Saturday."

Harold agreed. "Are you able to stand on your own?"

"Oh. Yeah." The stranger pushed away slowly. When his hands left Harold's chest, Harold regretted their leaving. "It was the sudden movement I wasn't ready for." He ran a hand through his hair. "I think I drank more last night than I realized."

"That's usually the case when you end up passing out in a cardboard box."

"Save people like this often, do you?" His lips quirked into a smile. Harold recognized that smile. With his hair brushed out of his face, Harold could see the equally familiar warm chocolate eyes. He'd not forgotten those eyes.

If this is how karma works, I'll miss planes for the rest of my life.

"Taylor?"

Taylor blinked, swayed a bit, then furrowed his brow. "You're the guy from the plane. Ha...oh shit, I know this. Ha..."

"Harold." Harold tried hard not to feel offended. Truth be told, he hadn't expected Taylor to remember him at all.

"Right! I knew that. Honestly. It's the hangover."

"Sure." Harold told himself the fact that Taylor knew his name started with an *H* was impressive enough. He shouldn't feel hurt. "Come on, let's get you inside."

"Well, now I feel better knowing I'm not entering the den of a complete stranger," Taylor said cheerfully. "Oh wait! My mask! Please tell me I didn't lose that too." His shoulders slumped.

Harold looked into the box. At the bottom was what looked like a 3D rendering of a dog's head out of leather or rubber. It was mostly black with gray on either side of the snout and above the eyes. He'd never seen anything like it before. "Do you mean that?"

"Yes! Thank goodness! That one is my favorite. It's really comfortable." Taylor tried reaching for it and groaned, putting a hand to his head. "Bending over is not in my near future."

"Noted." The word slipped from Harold's mouth before his mind could filter it. "Let me get it."

The box was too big to reach the bottom; he ended up lifting it and pouring the mask into Taylor's waiting grasp.

"Thank you!"

The bright smile Taylor shot his way did funny things to Harold's insides. *Easy, Harold. We already determined he's out of your league for a relationship, remember? And you're not made for a one-night stand.*

Who was he kidding? If he had any chance with Taylor, he'd jump on it in a second. "Let's get inside already."

He hadn't thought about what bringing Taylor inside his apartment building would be like until he'd already entered the lobby. Thankfully, only one person was exiting as they entered, but George was at the front desk like every weekend morning. He'd been there when Harold had left to get his groceries.

"Hey, George," Harold said with a smile and a wave, pretending there wasn't a man with no pants following closely behind him.

"Morning, Harold. It's a beautiful day, isn't it?" George replied pleasantly, as if Taylor truly was invisible. Harold fell a little more in love with the staff of his building at that.

"Gorgeous," he replied and angled for the elevators.

They headed up to the seventh floor and made the short walk to Harold's front door without running into anyone else. Harold gestured for Taylor to go inside, locking the door behind them with a sigh of relief.

"Let me put this bag in the kitchen, and I'll get you

those pants," he said as he dropped his keys on the front table and turned on the lights.

"Thanks," Taylor said. It was almost a surprise to hear his voice.

"You all right?" Harold asked.

"Yeah, just felt a little like Vivian walking through the lobby."

Harold stopped walking. "As in *Pretty Woman*?"

"Yup."

"I'm surprised you know the movie."

Taylor smiled. "It's one of my mother's favorites."

Of course it was. "If I remember correctly, you're a photographer's assistant, not a prostitute."

Taylor gestured to himself. "Do I look like a photographer's assistant right now?"

"You don't look like a prostitute."

"And you know what one looks like?" Taylor asked.

No, Harold didn't, but all this talk about what Taylor looked like was making him all too aware of the man's bare legs and how enticing they were as they disappeared beneath his sweatshirt.

He swallowed. "How about I get you those pants?" he said, his voice a little rough.

Yes, pants would be good. Taylor didn't actually feel like a prostitute, but he had felt awkward walking through the lobby of Harold's apartment building. He could only dream of affording a place like this with its swanky modern hallways, discreet staff members, and view of Central Park at the end of the road. The floor tiles had been the kind that sounded like money when people walked on them. Even

Harold's simple shoes had the right pitch to belong there. Taylor, in his bare feet, definitely didn't.

His bare feet. Gross. He must have been blackout drunk to walk the streets of Manhattan barefoot. Where the hell were his shoes? And his phone, his wallet, and the rest of his clothes for that matter. Taylor hoped they were still at the dungeon where the party had been held. If so, he had a good chance of getting them back.

He needed to call Joanne as well. She was probably wondering where he was. She might have assumed he'd found someone to go home with last night, but he still needed to check in with her.

If only he had met someone. Instead, he'd been too busy thinking about Liam to play like he'd planned. When he'd been about to leave for the party, his ex had started asking questions.

"Where are you going?"

"Out."

"With who?"

"Does it matter?"

"I have a right to know."

"No, you don't. Liam, we're living together out of necessity. We're not dating anymore. We both agreed we'd be better off broken up."

"You agreed."

Oh fuck. Please no. *"You also agreed."*

"You gave me no choice!"

Taylor put a hand to his head. He didn't need this. Not now. He'd finished work and was home. He could finally play. He wasn't going to let Liam spoil his pup time. He needed it. *"Can we talk about this later?"*

"Sure. Go ahead. Have fun fucking around on me."

Taylor hadn't dignified that with a response. He'd

grabbed his mask and keys and headed out, but the conversation had stayed with him, tainting his enjoyment of the party. There'd been plenty of fellow pups to play with and Masters both new and familiar he could have asked to scene with. Instead, he'd sat at the bar thinking about his situation with Liam.

They'd both agreed it was over. He was sure it was proximity and a lack of other options making Liam say otherwise. It'd been the same situation that had led them to date in the first place. Being together these last seven months had been a mistake, but they'd had no choice. Taylor couldn't wait until their lease was up and they could both move on. He wasn't looking forward to going home and continuing their conversation.

"Try these on."

Harold stood in front of him holding a pair of sweatpants. The man was about six inches taller than him with a wider frame. There was no way the pants would fit, but they had a pull tie, so there was a chance they'd stay up if he tied them tight enough.

"I also brought a T-shirt and a sweatshirt for you," Harold said. "They'll be big, but I figured they were better than nothing. There's a bottle of water in the fridge and aspirin in the cabinet if you'd like them."

"Thank you," Taylor said gratefully. "Would you mind if I used your bathroom to wash up?" He would not feel comfortable until he'd scrubbed his feet raw.

"Not at all. It's at the end of the hall."

Taylor took the clothes and headed for the bathroom. He didn't emerge until his skin was red from scalding heat and scouring. The clothes were as big as expected, but they were soft and comfortably worn in. He wanted to curl up inside them and sleep off the rest of his hangover. The temptation only strengthened as he joined Harold on the couch. He might not have recalled the man's name, but he definitely remembered wanting to snuggle and be petted by him. Something about the man called to his inner pup. The way he looked strong and tough, and the contrast of his kindness.

If only he were kinky.

"Coffee's brewing," Harold said. He gestured toward a bottle of water and some pills on the coffee table. "And I thought you might want these."

"You're a god."

"Is it that easy to become one?"

"Right now, yes."

Taylor knocked back the pills and chased them down with swigs of the water. The bottle was cold, fresh from the fridge, and he pressed it against his forehead.

"Mind if I ask what happened?" Harold said softly. "It's not every day I find someone in your predicament outside my apartment."

"And here I thought you did this all the time." Taylor sighed and put the bottle down. "I can't believe I slept in a box like a dog left on the side of the road."

"Well..." Harold eyed Taylor's mask. It was currently facing them on the coffee table.

"Does it bother you?" Taylor asked. His back tingled with the instinctual creeping of wariness he always got when he didn't know someone's perception of kink and was about to find out.

"I don't know enough to be bothered."

"Usually it's the people who don't know enough that are bothered."

Harold shrugged.

That's it? That was unexpectedly chill of him. Taylor

let out another sigh and sank back into the couch cushions. "All I wanted to do last night was unwind."

"Blacking out in a cardboard box isn't unwound enough for you?"

"Not that kind of unwind. Last night I finally had some time to be *me*. To just...let go. I've been waiting all week for it, and I let the opportunity slip through my fingers."

"And the mask is a part of that?"

Taylor hesitated, some of his unease returning. Harold had said he didn't know enough to be bothered. Would telling him more change his mind? Taylor had liked him when they'd met on the plane. The man's kindness today had only strengthened his opinion. He hoped Harold's reaction to kink wouldn't prove his judgment misplaced.

"Yeah," Taylor said. "When I'm a pup, I can relax, have someone pet me. Tell me I'm a good boy. That I've done well, worked hard." He ached as he listed the simple pleasures he'd been longing for. It'd been the reward he'd promised himself, and he still wanted it.

"That's it?"

"That's it."

"I can do that."

That was the last thing Taylor had expected Harold to say.

As if realizing his own words, Harold backtracked. "I mean, it's so simple. Anyone can do that."

"Not anyone," Taylor said.

"No, I suppose not." After a moment of silence, Harold added, "But I can. If you want."

Taylor wanted that more than words could say. The thought alone rushed the power of speech right out of his head. All he could do was nod. *Please,* he begged, hoping his eyes conveyed his yearning.

Harold studied him for a moment and then shifted on his end of the couch. "Here, boy," he said, patting his leg.

Taylor's eyes widened. *Is this really happening?* He moved forward onto his hands and knees and crawled the short distance to put his head in Harold's lap. Harold's leg was warm against his cheek. It felt nice. He thought of his mask, but Harold's fingers were in his hair before he could ask for it. Within moments his eyes were closing, and his body sank into the cushions.

"That's it. Just rest for a bit."

The gentle petting of his hair was hypnotic. Slowly, the work chatter in his mind quieted. The stress from the past week lifted and dispersed like dust in a soft breeze.

"Good boy."

Harold's voice was deep and steady, an anchor as he began to float. It was a sexy voice, made for soothing and giving orders. Taylor would love to hear it tell him to come.

"Hush now. Relax and let me pet you."

Oh, that was good. Guidance. His mind had wandered, hadn't it? Taylor drew his attention inward, to the sensations in his hair and the comfort of the couch. Was Harold enjoying this? He certainly was. He really hoped Harold wasn't finding it weird.

"Your mind is running like a rodent on a wheel," Harold said. "I can feel you twitching with every thought. How are you going to unwind if it's so noisy in there?"

I'm sorry. I don't know why I can't make it stop. It's usually not this hard to make it stop. Taylor whimpered.

Harold was quiet for a time, and the worry that had been budding in Taylor's brain threatened to blossom. Then Harold took hold of his chin and turned his head to face him.

"You've worked hard this week, but the week is over.

There is nothing you need to do right now except lie on this couch and be petted. This is your reward, Taylor. Take it."

Ah. Permission. He hadn't thought to ask for it, and yet it was given. Taylor nestled his cheek back onto Harold's thigh and closed his eyes. This time when the strands of his hair were gently stroked, he had no issue drifting away.

Chapter Three

Harold couldn't stop running his fingers through Taylor's hair. It was much softer than dog fur and as pleasant to pet. His thigh was warm where Taylor's cheek rested against it. He remembered feeling a similar heat when Missy had lain like this. Though, in Missy's case, the sensation had sometimes been accompanied by drool. The moment was so reminiscent of evenings he'd spent with Missy that an ache clenched in his chest, and he had to blink the sting from his eyes.

Perhaps that was the reason he'd offered to do this for Taylor. He'd originally done so on a whim, wanting more attention from the hot man currently resting in his lap. Now, as the silence of the room permeated his thoughts and the warmth of Taylor's body reminded him of company, he knew whatever his reasons, at the heart of it all had been loneliness. To do this for Taylor meant stealing a few more moments with him, and Harold was greedy for that time because when it was done, he would be alone in his apartment once again.

He brushed the strands of hair around Taylor's ear, glad

he'd done this and not only for the companionship. When Taylor had spoken of his interests, he'd done so with such yearning. It'd been written all over his face. Now that he'd gotten what he'd longed for, he was happy. Even as he dozed, he was smiling.

Harold liked seeing that smile on Taylor's face and putting it there hadn't been as weird as he'd thought it would be. Maybe because there hadn't been much "dog" to the situation.

No, that wasn't true. Even without the mask or anything visual, Taylor had been in a mindset before he'd fallen asleep. Harold had felt it. "Dog" had definitely been a part of what they'd done.

And yet it still hadn't been as weird as he'd thought it would be. The part that had bothered him the most was not knowing what to do. He'd basically acted like he would have for Missy. Overall, the mechanics had been the same, and it seemed to have worked out. Now all he had to do was wait for Taylor to wake up.

Taylor came back to awareness slowly. He lingered on the edge of wakefulness, taking in the quiet of the room and the plushness of the couch until he could convince himself to open his eyes. When he did, he was greeted by an unfamiliar room.

Even from his position, he could tell it was spacious. More so than his cramped apartment, though most of the claustrophobic feeling at home came from Liam's clothes all over the place. This room was neat and tidy, with recently polished wood floors and a big picture window through which he could see the apartment across the way. The furniture was also of a higher quality than his. The coffee table matched the couch and end chairs. His had been found on the side of the road. It was a solid piece of wood but was dwarfed by the massive couch he and Liam had purchased from a thrift shop.

Despite being in a new place, Taylor felt comfortable here. He stretched, the action more like a cat waking than a dog.

"You up?"

Harold. He recognized the voice. It had accompanied him as he'd floated, telling him he was good, and beautiful, and his hair was soft. Right now, he was drowsy, unfocused, and his mouth was stuck together. He nodded.

"It's time for lunch. Pizza okay?"

Taylor nodded again and eased himself into a sitting position. He still wasn't ready for words but sitting up was doable.

"I'm going to order us something and get you another bottle of water. You sit and take your time. Do you have any allergies I need to know about?"

Taylor shook his head.

"Good." Harold brushed a hand over his head and stood. "You did really well," he said before heading toward the kitchen.

The praise lit Taylor up from inside, and he smiled. He brought a hand up to his hair. He was sure Harold had petted him the entire time Taylor had been on his lap. And that wasn't the first accolade he'd given either. For someone who didn't know anything about pup play, Harold was a natural. The scene had been just what Taylor had been looking for. He felt lighter, refreshed, and less stressed than he had in weeks.

He stretched and collapsed back against the cushions.

Harold had the potential to be a really good Master and given the fantasies Taylor had been picturing him in since they'd met, the idea was a dangerously appealing one.

He did it one time. Don't get your hopes up for a repeat performance. Just file this away for replay later tonight.

But they were having lunch together. That meant Harold wasn't kicking him out any time soon. He wondered when Harold would start hinting it was time to go. It wasn't like he'd planned on having Taylor as a guest. What had his plans been for the weekend?

It didn't matter. Taylor would enjoy the time while it lasted. It'd been worth it so far.

———

In the kitchen Harold stood dazed, his cell phone forgotten in his hand. He'd gotten as far as pulling the number for his favorite pizza place up on the screen before reality hit him. He'd been fine with what he'd done with Taylor, but he hadn't thought about what happened after Taylor woke up.

Taylor hadn't replied verbally to any of Harold's questions. Did that mean he was still in "dog" mode? Did he expect Harold to do more? They hadn't talked about doing anything else. Should Harold continue treating him like a dog or was that over? What was he supposed to do?

He was totally out of his depth.

Not only that, but Harold suddenly remembered all the things he'd said when Taylor was a "dog." He'd complimented him, told him he was a good boy, and beautiful, and all sorts of other embarrassing things. He hoped Taylor had been as zoned out as he'd looked. If he was lucky, Taylor hadn't heard any of it. If Taylor had, Harold hoped he never found out.

Maybe he shouldn't have offered to get pizza. No, he didn't want Taylor to go yet. A part of him didn't want Taylor to go at all.

He took a deep breath and let it out slowly. "I can do this," he whispered to himself. "It's just pizza. I'll order and go back out there and take it one step at a time."

He pressed dial. While the phone rang, he wondered what Taylor would like, but he didn't want to burden him with talking. In the end, he went with his default choice: mushrooms and sausage. If Taylor didn't like it, hopefully he wouldn't mind picking them out of the cheese.

After confirming the price, giving his credit card number, and acknowledging the half hour wait for food, Harold grabbed two bottles of water and took another deep breath. He could handle this. It didn't matter if Taylor was up for talking or not. He'd figure it out.

First things first. He returned to the living room and handed over one of the bottles of water. Taylor looked grateful as he took it, but he still moved a little groggily. Harold drank half of his own water before setting it on the coffee table and dropping back onto the couch.

"Are you all right?" he asked once Taylor was done drinking. He'd nearly finished the bottle.

Taylor nodded.

Still not talking then. "Want me to put on a movie?" Then they wouldn't have to talk at all.

Taylor looked at him and smiled softly. He nodded again, probably more for Harold's benefit than any desire to watch something. Harold pulled up Netflix and turned on the first suggestion in the For You section, not bothering to see what it was. It ended up being some over-the-top modern comedy he had no interest in. That was often the case with his Netflix queue. He let random things run as background noise when he was working. It had to be something he wouldn't be distracted by, so they were usually from genres he didn't care for. This created a varied watch history of stuff he didn't like for the recommendation algorithm to work from, which meant anything Netflix suggested was most likely something he'd never want to see.

Forty-five minutes later, the pizza arrived. Harold answered the door and when he returned, Taylor asked, "Are you okay?" He looked more alert and attentive than before.

"Me?" Harold asked.

"I was wondering what you thought of..."

Oh. Harold set the pizza down on the table. "I'm not weirded out, if that's what you're worried about. It was fine. Nice, actually." For the most part. Afterward had been a little awkward. Kind of like the morning after a one-night stand, where you wonder if you should stay for breakfast or if you should have left the night before.

"Good." Taylor let out a relieved sigh.

Harold handed him a doubled-up paper plate and opened the pizza box. The aroma of all things delicious wafted toward them and both their stomachs growled.

"I hope you like mushrooms and sausage," Harold said.

"That's a literal question and not a euphemism, right?"

"What would mushrooms be a euphemism for?"

"I meant the sausage."

"I think it's been established we're both into the sausage euphemism."

Taylor grinned and reached for a slice of pizza.

"Was that what you were looking for?" Harold asked. "The..." He gestured, as if that would help him find the right word to describe what he'd done.

"Scene. It's called a scene, and yes. You gave me exactly what I was looking for. Thank you."

Taylor sounded more grateful than he needed to be. It wasn't like Harold had done much. At least, he hadn't thought he had. He didn't understand enough to know for sure.

"I'm glad," he said.

"Are you?" Taylor asked. "You look confused."

"I can be both." Harold reached for his own slice of pizza.

"True. Did you want to ask me anything?"

"As long as you're happy with what happened, I'm not sure there's anything to ask."

"There's plenty to ask! You just had your first pup play scene. How can you not have questions?"

"That's what it's called?"

Taylor rolled his eyes. "What was that about not having questions?"

Harold shrugged. "I don't know what questions to ask."

"You can ask whatever you want."

"Right now, I want to eat. Can we do that and field the questions later?"

"Sure."

They dug in. The pizza was fresh from the oven and delivered fast enough that the cheese was still ooey-gooey delicious. It stretched for miles, just like Harold liked it.

"Mmm," Taylor moaned in approval. "I just seared my mouth, but I don't care. This is so good."

"I know. Too bad I didn't think to get garlic knots. They make them the size of your fist."

Taylor groaned. "I'm already foodgasming over here. No need to help."

Harold laughed. "How about a distraction, then? Want to watch a movie?"

"As long as it's not the one you had on before."

"God yes. Any preference?"

"Anything but that one."

Harold laughed again and put on the first superhero film he came across.

They continued eating, and Taylor managed to keep his enthusiasm quiet while an ordinary boy began his journey of transformation. As the first film ended and the sequel began, Taylor set his empty plate aside and turned to Harold, biting his bottom lip. "Can I put my head in your lap again?"

"Sure." Harold wiped his fingers clean and moved his own plate out of the way.

The weight of Taylor's head on his thigh was welcome, as if his leg had been lonely without it. Though Harold turned his attention back to the movie, he couldn't help idly running his fingers through Taylor's hair like he had before. They watched the whole trilogy like that, and when it ended it was dinner time.

Taylor sat up. "I should probably go."

Harold didn't get a chance to process his disappointment before it was swamped by horror. Taylor had a boyfriend. He lived with him, for Christ's sake! What the hell had he been doing all day petting someone else's boyfriend? Better yet, why had Taylor felt the need to go out and find someone to do that for him when he had a boyfriend at home?

"Right," Harold said, his voice catching in his throat. "Your boyfriend's probably worried by now."

Taylor visibly deflated. He hadn't looked that lost when he'd been hungover in the cardboard box.

"Is everything all right?" Harold asked.

"Yeah. I'm just...not looking forward to going home."

"Trouble in paradise?"

"We're not really dating. We broke up two months ago. The only reason we're still living together is because we can't afford to break our lease."

Wait, Taylor's single? And he'd been single when we met on the plane? "Is it really that bad?" Harold asked, trying to sympathize while elation bubbled in his chest.

"He's the reason I got so drunk last night," Taylor said. "We got into an argument when I was leaving for the party, and I ended up brooding over it rather than enjoying myself."

A party where people wore dog masks and asked for petting. And probably more. Harold was reasonably sure pup play incorporated more than lying on a couch. He really should do as Taylor had suggested and ask those questions, but right then he had more pressing concerns. Mainly the fact that the really, really hot guy in his apartment was single and didn't want to go home.

"You don't have to go," he said. "Why not stay for dinner? There's plenty of pizza left."

The thought of not going home made Taylor ache. He would much prefer to stay here with Harold and his gentle hands and comfortable couch. It was only postponing the inevitable, but the offer was too strong a temptation to resist.

"As long as you don't mind," he said.

"Not at all."

They reheated the pizza and started another movie. The cheese was less stretchy the second time around but still delicious. And as if it were already routine, after they finished eating, Taylor laid his head back in Harold's lap and Harold petted him.

I could get spoiled like this, Taylor thought.

Harold's fingers didn't stay only in his hair. They caressed the shell of his ear, sending pleasant shivers down his body. They danced over the side of his neck, thumb pressing lightly as if to massage. The sensations set Taylor's nerves alight.

Taylor was perfectly content in this moment of comfort and sweet torture. Not wanting to give Harold any reason to change it, he moved his top leg a little higher to hide his body's reaction.

Chapter Four

Taylor fell asleep on Harold's lap, and when he woke it was morning. Panicked, he shot up into a sitting position, jamming the back of his head into Harold's chin.

"Ow!" they both exclaimed, putting a hand to their respective injuries.

"Well, good morning to you too," Harold said.

"Thank goodness your jaw is padded," Taylor said. "I would have been impaled otherwise."

"Are you suggesting I have a pointy chin?"

"I don't know. I can't see it." Taylor rubbed the back of his head where it ached and flinched. The spot was tender. "From the wound it left behind, I'm thinking yes."

"I will have you know my jaw is not pointy. It is chiseled and makes me look ruggedly handsome."

Taylor couldn't argue. Harold was handsome. "Then why do you hide it?"

Harold drew back as if affronted. "My beard doesn't hide anything. It emphasizes my good looks."

Taylor couldn't argue with that either. He liked Harold's beard, but it was fun teasing him. "Is that so?"

"You dare to insult my beard?" Harold asked. "And here I was thinking I'd brew up some nice coffee to get the day started. Forget it. You're getting instant."

"I like instant, thank you very much."

"Then you're getting decaf."

Taylor gasped in horror, which was mostly genuine. You didn't mess with a person's coffee. "You monster! I'm the victim here. I'm still seeing stars."

"Excuse me? I'm the victim. You hit me, not the other way around."

"Technically, we hit each other," Taylor pointed out. "So says Newton."

"You're still getting instant coffee."

"As long as it's not decaffeinated."

Harold rose from the couch to, Taylor presumed, make said coffee. Taylor followed him into the kitchen, trying to determine if he were dizzy from the impact. Thankfully, no.

"Do you even have decaf?"

"No. I don't have fancy coffee either. Actually"—Harold rummaged in a cabinet—"I lied. I have the fancy shit. Madeline sent it to me as a gift once."

"How old is it?"

Harold shrugged and chucked it back into the cupboard. "No idea. I never think to make it when I want coffee."

In minutes they had steaming mugs in their hands, and Taylor couldn't have cared less that it wasn't the fancy stuff.

"Do you do breakfast?" Harold asked.

"When I have time."

"How do you feel about eggs and bacon?"

"We're talking literally again, yeah?" Taylor teased.

"Yes," Harold said with a roll of his eyes, but he was smiling.

Taylor was a little in awe at how not awkward the morning was, especially when neither of them had planned on him staying over. He was grateful, though. He hadn't wanted to go home last night, and although he knew he'd have to eventually, he'd enjoy this time with Harold as long as he could.

"I feel very positively about them," Taylor said. "Especially when the eggs are over easy and toast is involved."

"That can be arranged." Harold opened a cabinet and took out a couple of pans.

"Do you need any help?" Taylor asked.

"Nah. If you want to grab a shower while you're waiting, you're welcome to."

"Are you politely telling me I stink?"

"No, I'm politely being a polite host." Harold gestured back toward the living room. "Towels are in the cabinet on the wall in the bathroom."

"See? That sounds like subtle insistence on my showering. You think I smell."

"I'm planning on taking a shower as well. I thought you might like your eggs before I did that."

Taylor had a better idea. "They say the best way to conserve water is with group showers."

"What study said that?"

"The one done by Professor Humpsalott from Dixie Wrecked University."

Harold laughed. "What are you, ten? You were so peacefully obedient as a dog. What happened?"

Taylor grinned. "If I were a dog, you'd have to wash me."

The humor in Harold's face morphed into something much more intensely focused. Taylor's body flushed hot beneath Harold's stare. "Do you like that idea?" he asked, his heartbeat quickening.

"Maybe," Harold said, but his tone implied yes.

The semi-erection Taylor had fallen asleep with came back in full. "You can if you want." *Please, please want to.*

Harold licked his lips. He wanted to. He really, really wanted to. Pup play included things like this? What else was involved? Was sex? If Harold gave in to washing Taylor, he was sure sex would end up on the table. At least he hoped it would. Was that something Taylor wanted from him?

They'd been flirting and teasing all weekend, but this was unfamiliar territory. If it'd been a simple one-night stand sort of thing, he'd know what was up. What were the rules here?

They'd returned to the questions he'd put off asking, but now was not the time, when he was thinking more with his dick than his brain. He took a step back, needing physical distance to help him clear his mind of the temptation that was Taylor.

"Maybe next time," he said. "You hop in first, and I'll get breakfast started. I'll also find more clean clothes you can wear."

"These are fine." Was that disappointment in Taylor's voice? "The towels are in the cabinet, you said?"

"Yeah. Use whatever you find."

"Thanks."

Then Harold and his eager cock were alone in the kitchen, trying to ignore the regret of a lost opportunity. He took a deep breath and turned back to the stove. "Eggs, Harold. Eggs. Bacon. Toast. You can do this."

His body moved on autopilot while the rest of his attention was tuned toward the bathroom and any sound of Taylor's movements. It was nice having someone in the apartment again, Taylor especially. The atmosphere felt lighter, more comfortable. Last night he'd slept better than he had in a while. He attributed that to the company.

Taylor's shower was quick but long enough to provide Harold with a full mental image of what his body might look like dripping with water and haloed in steam. The distraction made Harold burn his bacon.

"That looks flavorful," Taylor said when he saw it.

"What can I say? I like my breakfast with some heat."

Taylor slowly ran his tongue over his top lip. "Is that so?"

That mouth could bring a man to his knees if he hadn't already been sitting. "Eat your eggs before they get cold," Harold said.

Taylor pouted and did as he was told. He took each bite in the most seductive way possible. It was a relief when Harold finally made his escape into the bathroom for his shower. He used the opportunity for some much-needed tension relief.

He tried not to think of Taylor, but it was impossible after all their flirting. Why hadn't he asked those questions when Taylor had suggested it? Would he get another chance to? Last night Taylor had been reluctant to return to his apartment. That didn't mean he wanted to spend the whole weekend together. As Harold finished dressing and returned to the living room, a part of him expected to find Taylor ready to leave.

To his surprise, Taylor was snuggled under a blanket on the couch with the TV remote in hand. "Do you have any plans for today?" he asked.

"Nothing beyond laundry and vacuuming."

"Oh." Taylor put the remote down and shifted the blanket off his lap. "I shouldn't keep you from your errands."

"I would happily put them off for all eternity, if possible," Harold admitted.

Amusement curved Taylor's lips. "Not a fan of laundry?"

"It's not the laundry. It's the folding."

"Really? I like folding. It's meditative."

Was he crazy? "You're welcome to fold my laundry any day."

Taylor smirked. "Underwear too?"

Harold laughed. He'd fallen right into that trap.

"I don't mind folding if you don't mind the company," Taylor said.

It sounded like he still didn't want to go home. Harold didn't mind. Taylor was welcome to stay the day. The night too if he wanted.

"Be my guest," Harold said.

They did more than laundry. While the first load was running, Taylor dusted and Harold vacuumed. The help was wonderful, but how bad must things be at Taylor's apartment for the younger man to want to spend his day cleaning someone else's home?

"What did you have planned for today?" Harold asked.

"Doing my own laundry," Taylor said.

"Don't you think you should do it before the workweek begins?"

Taylor sighed. "Yeah, but I'm chicken. I don't want to bump into my ex at home, so I'm procrastinating."

"My shelves thank you, but you can't put it off forever."

"No? And here I thought I'd move in like a stray."

"Isn't that up to the owner of the place?"

Taylor shook his head. "You're an animal lover. You can't say no." And to emphasize the truth of his statement, he looked at Harold with wide sad eyes. Harold felt himself caving like he would have for Missy as he looked into them. He turned away.

"That's freaky. You're not a dog. You shouldn't be able to pull a stunt like that."

Taylor grinned.

"You have work tomorrow, don't you?" Harold asked. "You can't go to work in my clothes."

Taylor's smile faded. "Are you kicking me out?"

Was he? Yes. Because if Taylor didn't leave now, Harold might be tempted to keep him like a stray.

Apparently, his mouth wasn't hooked up to the logical part of his brain. "No. I'm telling you, you need clothing that fits you for work tomorrow. You might as well suck it up, get your clothes, and bring them here. We're already doing laundry."

Taylor stared at him, his mouth agape. "What?"

Harold didn't understand either. He just knew he didn't want Taylor to leave. Not yet. "Stay here. Stray or not, you obviously don't want to go home, so stay until your lease is up and you can find your own place."

***

"What?" Taylor said again, still uncomprehending.

"You heard me."

"Yeah." But who offered to let someone they'd only known for twenty-four hours move in? Even if it was temporary. "You don't even know how long I've got left on my lease."

"How long?"

"Five weeks."

Harold shrugged. "Look, I'm not offering much. Just a foldout couch and some space from your ex."

"What's the catch?" Taylor asked. There had to be a catch.

"Clean up after yourself, do the dishes, and fold the laundry."

"I'm not a charity case." Yeah right. He'd seen the gorgeous lobby downstairs and the view of Central Park. This place was so out of his league. He'd never be able to afford to live somewhere like this.

"I'm not trying to make you feel like one." Harold sighed. "You seem reluctant to go home, and I have an empty couch, so I thought I'd offer you a place away from your ex if you wanted one. That's all."

It was a really nice offer, and Taylor was strongly tempted by it. Harold was right; he didn't want to go home. "Can I buy you dinner as a thank you?"

"Sure."

Taylor found himself speechless again. Was he really agreeing to move in with Harold for a month? "Are you sure about this?"

"No," Harold admitted, which, if he were being honest, made Taylor feel a little better. "But so far things have worked better with you if I don't think too much before I do them."

Taylor didn't know if that was good or bad, but he decided to take it. "I should get my clothes then."

"Do you want me to go with you?"

"No, I can do it." He didn't want Harold to meet Liam. Harold was like an oasis. He didn't want that feeling tainted by the stress of his previous relationship. He also didn't want to hear what Liam would say about Taylor "bringing another man home," especially after his accusations.

He got up to leave and then remembered he didn't have anything on him. No cell phone, no wallet, no keys. "Can I borrow your phone for a minute?"

"Sure." Harold handed his cell over. "You can use my bedroom for privacy."

"Thanks."

He made his way into the bedroom and closed the door. Since he had no idea what Joanne's phone number was, he logged into his account on Harold's Facebook Messenger app and called her that way.

"Where have you been?" she shouted as soon as she saw him. "I've been worried sick about you. I even called Liam to find out where you were."

"You called Liam?" *Shit.* He'd been planning on saying he'd slept at Joanne's to avoid any more accusations of cheating from his ex. Now what was he going to do?

"What else was I supposed to do? You weren't answering your phone."

"That's because I left my phone at the party, along with my wallet and my clothes."

She gasped. "What the hell happened to you? Are you all right?"

"I'm fine. I'm actually heading home now. It's the reason I called. Would you be able to get my stuff from Andriy and meet me in front of my building?" Andriy was the owner of the dungeon the party had been at.

"Of course. I'll call him immediately and make sure he

found everything." For a moment, he thought he was in the clear. Then her brows furrowed. "Wait, if you haven't been home yet, where have you been?" He could see her searching the background for clues. Her eyes narrowed when she realized he was in a bedroom. "Do not tell me I freaked out for nothing and you've been with some guy this whole time."

"Not in the way you think," Taylor said. "I got drunk that night, and I must have taken a walk. I ended up passed out in some trash outside some guy's apartment building. He took me in and helped me clean up. In fact, I'm wearing his clothes right now because the only thing I have of my own is a G-string." And a pup mask. Should he leave it or take it with him when he left? What if Harold changed his mind while Taylor was gone? He didn't want to lose it.

"Taylor! How could you be so careless? And who is this guy?"

"Just some guy. No one you know."

"He must be more than some guy if you slept at his place last night."

"He let me crash on the couch when I didn't want to go back home."

"Setting aside all the questions that statement gives me, what happened with Liam? He's the reason you didn't go home, isn't he?"

"He accused me of planning to cheat on him when I left on Friday. He also said he didn't want to break up."

She rolled her eyes. "What is wrong with him? You both know it's over. It's been that way for months."

He opened his mouth to reply, but she kept going.

"And you. What is wrong with you? You should have found me at the party on Friday and told me all this then!

We could have drunk together, eaten junk food, and vented it all out. In a nice, safe place called my apartment."

"I didn't want to ruin your night."

"If you were in my presence right now, I would kick you so hard."

"I know, I know. I just…"

"Didn't want to ruin my night, so you decided not to tell me what was going on?" she asked, her tone acerbic. "Instead, I got to panic for a good twenty-four hours when I couldn't find you yesterday. You could have been dead in a ditch somewhere or kidnapped by human traffickers."

"You didn't think I was kidnapped by traffickers."

"Not the point, Taylor."

He knew what the point was, but when he was in one of those moments, guilt overrode logic. He hated the thought of burdening her.

She sighed. "I'm glad you're okay."

"Me too."

"Am I dropping off the keys, or should I prep for moral support?"

"Moral support and a few lies?"

"I'm listening."

"I'd hoped to tell Liam I stayed at your place this weekend. Now I don't think I can do that."

She shrugged. "We'll say I found you, and it was a false alarm."

"How the hell is that going to work?"

She waved away his concerns. "Is that the only thing?"

"I'd like to tell him I'm staying with you for a while longer."

"You're moving in with the guy who found you in the trash?"

It sounded so much better when he was a lost pup in a

box. "Not moving in. Just crashing until I can get a new place."

"That's moving in, Taylor."

"Are you going to cover for me or not?"

"I will, but you're going to let me take you to this guy's house so I can vet him. I want photographic evidence of who he is before he locks you in his dungeon and I never see you again."

"He doesn't have a dungeon."

"That's what they all say."

"Not in our circles."

She laughed.

"Really, though, he doesn't have a dungeon. He's not kinky. He's just some guy."

"And yet, you're moving in with him."

"A nice guy who will let a near stranger sleep on his couch."

"This is not alleviating my worry," Joanne said.

"Would it help if I said I'd met him before?"

"You didn't think to lead with that?"

"It's not much better. He's the guy I sat next to on the plane from Minnesota on Monday."

"The hot Daddy you flirted with?" she asked, her eyes alight with excitement.

"Yeah."

"This is better than a dungeon! It's a fucking romance novel!"

"Last time I checked, your romance novels included dungeons."

She waved his words away. "Not the point. This is totally the setup for a romance. And now you're moving in with him!" She inhaled sharply. "Is there only one bed?"

"The couch is a foldout."

"You're not sleeping on the couch."

"I did last night." He neglected to tell her Harold had been on it with him.

"That's temporary. Trust me, Taylor. That Daddy of yours isn't going to resist you for long if you're in close quarters."

"He's not a Daddy. I don't want a Daddy."

"Then let me have him."

"No." The word came out sharper than he intended. "Sorry."

"Yeah, that's what I thought," she said smugly. "We'll see how long you sleep on that couch. Now I really want to meet him."

Taylor didn't have the brain power to entertain her fantasies right then. "How about we get through step one first? I still need my stuff to get into my apartment."

"I'll be there in an hour."

He hung up, logged out, and headed back into the living room to return Harold's phone. "Thank you."

"No problem."

"Mind if I ask for another favor?"

"What do you need?"

Taylor bit his lip. "Money for the subway. I'll pay you back once I have my wallet."

"That's fine. I can afford the three dollars."

This was so embarrassing. "Thank you."

After also borrowing a coat, an oversized pair of flip-flops, and figuring out directions to the nearest subway station, Taylor headed toward the door.

"You're coming back, right?" Harold asked.

The question flooded Taylor with reassurance he hadn't known he needed. A part of him feared Harold would change his mind as soon as Taylor was out of sight. Maybe

Harold was afraid of the same thing. "As long as you still want me to," he said.

"Good."

"Good."

No longer feeling embarrassed, Taylor left with a silly little smile on his face that stayed even after he'd boarded the subway train.

Chapter Five

This was insane. What the fuck was he doing letting some stranger stay with him? Harold picked up the phone. He should call his sister. She'd talk sense into him. *What if she succeeds?* He put the phone down and sank onto the couch.

"What is wrong with me?"

The dog mask on his coffee table didn't answer. It stared at him, the empty eye sockets lifeless yet judgmental.

"Taylor's a cuter dog than you." He glared at it, then turned it to face the other way. "Oh my god, what is *wrong* with me?"

He persisted for about ten minutes before he gave in and called his sister.

"Emergency, crisis, advice, or you love me?" she asked in lieu of a greeting.

"What's the difference between the first two?"

"Emergency means someone's dying, bleeding out, or a hospital is otherwise involved. Crisis is...a crisis."

"So glad you didn't follow the path to becoming an English teacher like you wanted in fifth grade. I would pity your students with explanations like that."

"They'd still answer the question."

"Crisis."

"What have you done? Please tell me you haven't gotten back with your ex."

"Uh, no. Why would you even think of that?"

"You don't call me about crises. I assumed you'd made a dumb decision."

"Like getting back together with Sean?"

"Yes, because that would be a bad decision of epic proportions. The man was a bore."

That was unfair. Sean had been a nice guy. Even when he'd wanted to break up, there'd been no fights or drama, just a straightforward conversation about how things weren't working.

That probably said a lot about their relationship.

"Outside the bedroom, maybe," Harold said.

As expected, his sister didn't let him off easy. "And inside?"

He couldn't flat-out lie to her, so he said nothing.

"That's what I thought. You need some excitement, little brother. Is this crisis of yours exciting?"

That was one way of putting it. "He's hot, he's sexy, he's too young for me, and I've asked him to move in. Temporarily. As roommates. Oh, and I've only been with him for twenty-four hours."

"Why is it temporary?" she asked.

"Have you been listening? I've only known the guy a day, and you're focusing on the deadline and not the moving in?"

"Harold, you wouldn't let someone move in unless you were sure about it. You're not impulsive."

"How does twenty-four hours not spell impulsive?"

"Are you trying to get me to disapprove of this?" she asked.

"No. Maybe. I don't know." He ran a hand over his face. "I don't know what I'm doing. This is unlike me."

"Maybe that's a good thing. You could use a little change in your routine."

"I'm trying to decide if I'm offended by that."

"Why is the situation temporary?" Madeline asked.

"I told him he could stay with me until his current lease is up. He didn't want to go home since he shares the apartment with his ex."

"Recent ex?"

"Recent enough."

"Aw, don't be the rebound guy."

"I can't be the rebound guy if it's just a temporary roommate thing."

"Like hell it's a temporary roommate thing. What was all that about hot and sexy? This situation is a porno waiting to happen."

"Did I mention he's kinky?"

"Oh, Harold! Fuck it. Be the rebound guy. Rebound the shit out of this man."

It took so little to change her mind. "You don't even know what kind of kinky."

"If you're not already scared off, it's not anything I'd disapprove of. And honestly, you could use some kinky in your life. Like I said, Sean was boring. He made you kind of boring too."

"I can feel the love," Harold said. "Unlikely potential for sex aside, I'm not crazy letting a complete stranger move in with me?"

"Unlikely, my ass," she muttered. "Are you so sure he's a stranger?"

"I told you I only just met him."

"That's not what I mean. It doesn't necessarily take a long time to get to know someone. Sometimes you just feel it."

Did he feel it? Harold thought of the comfortable time he'd shared with Taylor on the couch, the easy rapport they'd had when doing laundry, the fear that Taylor wouldn't return once he'd left.

"No," Harold said. "He isn't a stranger."

"See? I told you, you don't make impulsive decisions. Are you feeling better now?"

"Surprisingly, yes."

"Then my job here is done. Crisis averted."

Harold still thought he was crazy for letting Taylor move in, but he was no longer freaking out about it. "Thanks, sis."

"Anytime. Oh, and send me a picture of this young hottie of yours. And his social media. I want to stalk him."

"I will do no such thing."

"Yeah, you will. Love ya." She hung up.

Harold hoped she'd forget about her demand, but he knew better. Thankfully, he didn't know Taylor's social media, so he wouldn't have to lie when she inevitably called him back to remind him about it.

A new worry crept in to replace the old one. He didn't have Taylor's phone number or access to any of his social media. What if something happened to him? What if he did change his mind about coming back? Harold had no way to contact him. If Taylor didn't return, Harold would never know the reason why.

It took Taylor an hour and twenty minutes to reach his apartment. He only tripped over the flip-flops three times on the way. Okay, four, but who was there to prove it?

Joanne was waiting for him with a shopping bag when he arrived. He assumed the bag held his stuff, but before he could ask, the door flew open and Liam stood before them. His caramel brown hair was pulled back into a short ponytail, a few strands having worked loose to frame the left side of his face. He was dressed in sweats and a T-shirt. *Off to the gym probably.* Liam looked at them, startled for a moment, and then narrowed his eyes.

"Where the hell have you been?" he asked. "And whose clothes are those?"

"What? No hello?" Taylor asked as he stepped inside. Joanne followed, with Liam bringing up the rear.

It was weird being in his own apartment again. There wasn't the sense of *home* one would normally expect when returning. Nothing had changed. The controllers for Liam's Xbox were on the floor, as if he'd paused mid-game and would return in a few minutes. They were always like that even if he hadn't played in a week. Random pieces of clothing were strewn about since Liam was the type who came home and shed things without putting them away. The bookcase was still overstuffed with books belonging to the two of them—that was going to be a nightmare to unravel when they both moved out. The sink was full of dishes waiting to be washed, and in the bedroom at the end of the hall, Taylor's bed was unmade.

That last was a surprise. Since they'd broken up, they'd taken turns switching between the bed and the couch. It was Taylor's week for the bed, and it had been neat when he'd left on Friday.

"You know I've been worried about you," Liam said.

"Joanne called when she couldn't find you, and then you don't show up for two days?"

"I can see how worried you are, Liam." Taylor gestured toward the bedroom. "When did you decide I wasn't coming home?"

Liam crossed his arms in front of his chest. "You've been gone for two days."

"So you decided to sleep in my bed?"

"It's my bed too, and why the fuck should I sleep on the couch when you're not here?"

"As *Burlesque* as this moment is," Joanne said, stepping in between them, "not the point, boys."

Taylor let out a huff and stalked down the hall to the bedroom.

"How was the party?" Liam called after him. "Must have been good since you didn't come home."

Taylor's anger flared even hotter. It'd been Liam's fault he'd had a shitty time on Friday. Then again, if he hadn't gotten drunk, he wouldn't have met Harold again.

"It was fine," he said. "Didn't really do much."

"You didn't play with anyone?"

"Wasn't in the mood." He grabbed a bag and started shoving clothes and essentials into it. He didn't need to take everything. It wasn't like he was moving in with Harold permanently. He'd come and get the rest of his stuff once he found a new place.

"What are you doing?" Liam asked from the doorway.

"I'm staying with Joanne for a few days."

"You just got home, and you're already leaving again?"

Taylor threw a T-shirt into the bag with more force than necessary. "What does it matter? You and I are stuck here together. We're not here by choice."

"You know, ever since we broke up, you've become a real asshole."

"Oh, now you admit we've broken up?" Taylor asked. "What happened to Friday when you were accusing me of cheating on you?"

"I didn't accuse you of cheating on me."

"You told me to have fun fucking around on you!"

"Boys!" Joanne yelled. "My god, it's like monitoring a pair of teenagers. If you can't say anything nice, then shut the fuck up."

Taylor went back to packing, and there was blessed silence in the apartment for a few minutes.

"Aren't you living with someone?" Liam asked Joanne. He'd never been one to endure quiet for long.

"I'm between housemates at the moment."

"What happened to the last one?"

"Our contract was up, and he moved on."

"What was this one?" Taylor asked.

Joanne was a pansexual switch with an interest in many difference aspects of kink. She found her sexual and kink outlets in short-term contracts, which occasionally gave her a roommate. "Twenty-four-hour service D/s for two weeks. It was like a vacation retreat for him, and I didn't have to do laundry or dishes."

Taylor smiled, recalling his conversation with Harold about laundry.

"You never told me whose clothes you're wearing," Liam said. "They're obviously not yours."

Not that it was any of Liam's business. "I borrowed them when I couldn't find mine. This may be New York, but I'm not walking the streets in a G-string." Middle-of-the-night shit-faced wandering aside.

"What about the guy they belong to?"

Taylor shrugged. "He doesn't mind." He threw another shirt into his bag and zipped it closed.

"Ready?" Joanne asked.

Taylor took another look at the bed. He didn't want his favorite blanket smelling like Liam.

He wanted it smelling like Harold.

That was not a train of thought he should be boarding, but if he were honest, Harold's place had felt more welcoming than this one, even though Taylor had been an unexpected guest. And now he would be an expected one. He was suddenly itching to return.

He pulled the blanket out from the tangle of sheets. "Ready."

"Taylor?" Liam called as they headed toward the door, all traces of attitude gone from his voice. "Are you coming back?"

Taylor sighed. "I'm not sure," he said honestly.

Liam looked at him, and Taylor could see the unspoken words in his expression. Liam didn't like to be alone. More than the loneliness, Taylor saw sadness, and he could relate to it. Even though they hadn't worked out as boyfriends, they'd started as friends. They were mourning more than one ending as they neared the end of their lease.

As if he knew Taylor understood, Liam nodded.

"See ya, Liam," Taylor said.

"Bye, Taylor."

Taylor forced himself not to look back as he left, Joanne right behind him.

As expected, Joanne insisted on coming with him to Harold's place. It was logical to have a friend know where he was staying and with who. Safe, sane, and consensual and all that. Totally worked for real life as well as kink.

Any sense of logic vanished when Harold opened the door. Taylor had forgotten how tall he was. And how broad. And how distinguished the dusting of gray in his hair and beard made him look. Taylor's mouth watered just looking at him. Then Harold smiled and Taylor's brain short-circuited completely, sending all of his body's functionality south. Joanne was right. He definitely wanted in Harold's bed. Fuck the foldout.

"Hi," Joanne said, holding out a hand toward Harold. "I'm Joanne, Taylor's best friend."

Yes. Right. Manners. "She helped bring my stuff." Could that have been any more obvious? Apparently not, since Joanne rolled her eyes at him.

"Come on in," Harold said.

They dropped Taylor's luggage next to the couch, and Taylor laid the blanket down on it.

"I have blankets you can use," Harold said.

"This one's my favorite. It's extra fuzzy."

"I have the same one in purple."

"Purple?"

"My sister took the brown one."

Taylor laughed. "You couldn't buy two brown ones?"

Harold shrugged. "We liked both colors."

"I want to see your purple blanket."

Joanne cleared her throat, reminding Taylor she was there.

"My apologies," Harold said. "Would you like something to drink?"

"That would be lovely. Seltzer or water, please."

"Coming right up." Harold headed for the kitchen.

"Taylor tells me you work in, oh wait, Taylor's told me

nothing about you." Although her words were meant for Harold, Joanne gave Taylor a pointed look while she spoke. "What is it you do, Harold?"

Taylor couldn't see Harold's face, but he heard amusement in his voice as he called back, "I'm a computer programmer."

"A computer programmer," she echoed. "Must be a steady job if you can afford to live on the Upper West Side."

"I do well enough," Harold replied as he returned with her water. He set the glass down on the coffee table in front of her. "And what is it that you do?"

"I'm a systems analyst for a small IT service and consulting company."

Harold's brows rose in surprise. "You must be good at your job. The systems analysts I've met are all at least ten years your senior."

"The benefit of having friends who start their own company right out of college," Joanne said with a grin. "What about family?"

"Family?"

"Do you have any?"

"I have a sister, brother-in-law, and a niece in Minnesota."

"That's far away. I'm guessing you don't get to see them very often."

"We talk a lot. Do video chats."

"Any boyfriends?"

"Not at the moment."

"Drinker?"

"When it suits."

"Prison record?"

"Okay," Taylor interrupted. "That's enough of an interrogation."

"One final question," Joanne said, holding up a finger. "Why have you invited my friend to live with you when you don't even know him? What's in it for you?"

The hint of a smile that had been curving Harold's lips as he fielded Joanne's questions faded. "Company," he said. "That's what's in it for me. I'd like the company. The rest is…" He shrugged. "Taylor wants to get away from his ex for a while, and I have an empty couch. It's as simple as that."

"So, you don't have ulterior motives to lock him away somewhere and inflict upon him the wonders of pain and ecstasy?"

Harold's brow furrowed. "No?"

"And you're not using him to pose as a significant other so you can join a swinger's club and explore the variety of multiple partners?"

"I don't share." Harold shook his head. "I mean, no."

Joanne leaned forward and narrowed her eyes, studying him. The action was almost comical and reminded Taylor of the chameleon in *Tangled* when they first met Flynn Rider in the tower.

"Okay," she said with a slap to her thighs. "That's good, then." She rose. "I'll leave you two to settle in." She turned to Taylor. "Walk me out?"

What just happened? Taylor followed her to the front door in a partial daze and continued to follow when she gestured for him to step into the hall.

"What was that?" he asked once the door was closed behind them.

"Vetting."

"Vetting is acting like an overprotective parent followed by an insane friend with fantastical delusions?"

"He didn't bat an eye at any of my questions, even the ridiculous ones." She started counting points on her fingers.

"He's got a steady job, a nice home"—she bumped his hip with hers—"he's single, and he totally looked taken aback when I asked if he was going to kidnap you, which, depending on your point of view, might not be in his favor. Overall, he seems like a good guy."

Leave it to Joanne to make a crazy interrogation lead to a totally reasonable conclusion.

"And," she added, stressing the word, "he's a wet dream of a Daddy. I want all the details."

Taylor snorted. "We'll see."

"You did catch the best part of what happened in there, didn't you?"

"What?"

She leaned close to him. "He said he doesn't share." She winked and skipped off down the hallway. Taylor barely registered her exit.

He doesn't share.

The words echoed in his head.

Please, oh please can he not share me?

"She seems nice," Harold said once Taylor had made his way back inside the apartment.

"She interrogated you."

"Out of concern for you," Harold pointed out.

"True. She is a really good friend. That's why I feel bad taking advantage of her kindness."

"How are you taking advantage of it?"

"She let me tell Liam I was staying with her."

"Why didn't you tell him you were staying here?" Was that disappointment in Harold's voice? Was it because Taylor lied or for something else?

"I didn't want him jumping to conclusions."

"The conclusion that you're moving in with someone else?"

"The conclusion that I'm seeing someone else."

"Ah, yes," Harold said, his voice hardened with sarcasm. "Because everything is perfectly platonic between us."

"What's that supposed to mean?"

Harold shook his head. "Nothing. You're welcome to tell your ex whatever you want."

Yes, he was. Why was Harold getting worked up about it? "Have you eaten? I'm starving."

Harold took a deep, slow breath before answering. "How do taquitos sound?"

"Where do you order from?"

"How dare you suggest such a thing. Mine are homemade."

Taylor's mouth watered for more than just the man standing across from him. "Homemade taquitos? Hell fucking yes, please."

Harold laughed, and the last of the awkward tension vanished. "Come on. You can be my sous-chef."

Harold was sure at least half the appreciative noises Taylor made over dinner sounded orgasmic on purpose.

"So, I shouldn't make these again?" he asked. "You've looked like you're in pain the whole time you've been eating them."

"I have not!" Taylor exclaimed. "That's the last time I compliment your cooking."

"Is that what that was supposed to be?"

Taylor stuck his tongue out at him and resumed eating. The honest pleasure in his expression as he chewed and swallowed was all the compliment Harold needed. He'd missed cooking for someone.

After dinner they sorted Taylor's things and threw them in the wash. While they were waiting for the cycle to finish, Harold made up the pullout bed with freshly laundered sheets.

"Pick whatever pillow and blankets you want," Harold said. "I have a collection."

"I'm fine with my blanket, but I'll take a pillow."

"Left closet in the foyer."

Taylor picked out a pillow, and they finished making the bed. Taylor even helped wash and dry the dishes. Their rhythm was strangely domestic as they sorted the apartment and got ready for the evening. It was an unfamiliar routine but more comfortable than Harold had anticipated. As Taylor transferred his clothing from the washer into the dryer, he thought about his sister's question. Was Taylor a stranger? Despite knowing nothing about him, Harold couldn't bring himself to change his answer: no.

By the time they were done, it was late and they both had work in the morning. Harold checked that Taylor didn't need anything, then headed to his room. He fell asleep still pondering the choice he'd made to live with someone else, if only for five weeks.

Monday came with an unsurprising bucketful of emails, issues, and questions on top of his planned to-do list. Harold dove into the workweek with his usual focus, not emerging for hours until the need for coffee and the fact his eyes were crossing forced him to step back from the computer. The apartment was strangely quiet as he filled his mug and returned to his laptop.

I can't be missing him already. He just left this morning.

Pushing the feelings aside, he woke the computer and dove back into the world of coding.

He was startled out of his concentration by the sound of

the front door opening. He'd given Taylor Sean's old keys. It would have been inconvenient if Taylor couldn't come and go as he pleased while they were living together.

Acquiring the keys had been an adventure. Harold had had to dig into the back of his closet where he'd stowed a box of things that reminded him of his ex to find them. At the time he'd hidden the box there, he'd been too emotional to let go. Then he'd forgotten about it. Now he'd taken the opportunity to finally throw the items inside away. It left him with a nice two-foot square of space in his closet, and he'd found an old CD he loved and hadn't listened to for years.

Taylor entered with a sigh and shrugged off his coat.

"Tough day?" Harold asked.

"A little."

"Give me twenty minutes and I'll start dinner."

Taylor nodded. "I'm gonna take a quick shower."

"Go ahead."

The shower seemed to wash the stress of Taylor's job off of him. He emerged looking much lighter in spirit and attractively damp. His T-shirt stuck to his chest in a few places, hinting that he hadn't been fully dry when he'd put it on.

"Feeling better?" Harold asked.

"Much," Taylor replied with emphasis.

"Dinner will be ready in half an hour. Can you make sure it doesn't burn so I can wash up too?"

"What do I have to do?"

"Not much. It's baking. Just take it out of the oven if the timer rings and I'm still not out."

"I can do that."

Despite Harold having a perfectly good table to eat dinner at, they ate on the couch again with a movie playing in the background. The rest of the week was much of the same. During the day they didn't see each other at all. Taylor left early every morning for his office or a photo shoot, and Harold stayed home and worked on a diminishing list of programming projects. At night they sat on the couch and watched movies or talked.

Harold learned Taylor was an only child who'd moved to New York from South Jersey for college and stayed after graduating. He had an aunt who lived in Jersey City, but the rest of his family was two hours away on a good day. He loved his job even though he wasn't in his goal position, but he was working on that. And some of his favorite things were strawberry ice cream, fizzy drinks, and snuggly blankets.

Even though he was getting to know Taylor, something was missing. The short conversations they had at night were all they had. After food, showers, and a little unwinding, they'd part ways for bed. Living together was brand new for them, yet Harold felt they were already stuck in a rut.

It wasn't like Taylor was a difficult roommate. He kept his stuff tucked into a corner of the living room, he was quiet in the mornings when their schedules didn't match, and he closed the foldout bed after waking. He wasn't picky when it came to food, he took reasonable-length showers, washed the dishes when Harold cooked, and was generally a neat person. Harold had nothing to complain about. In fact, he liked having Taylor's company in the house. He'd missed Missy but hadn't realized how lonely he'd been until there was another being in the apartment again.

So why was Harold frustrated?

His first theory was stress from lack of work. He had a solid group of clients but most of what he was doing for them lately was maintenance. His schedule was feeling a little empty, and he dreaded finding new work to fill it. That had always been the part of his job he'd hated the most, but the more he thought about it, the more he knew that wasn't the real problem.

Sex was next. It was a challenge not to push Taylor up against a wall when he came out of the bathroom with his hair tousled and wet from a shower, or when he walked around so casually in those sweatpants he slept in. They were soft and loose, and Taylor didn't wear a shirt to bed. Harold's mouth watered imagining that bare torso, smooth and muscular and perfect. He'd taken himself in hand every night since Taylor had moved in, but that was a frustration he knew. One he recognized, acknowledged, and grudgingly accepted. This was something else. Something pivotal, and Harold couldn't put a finger on it.

He figured it out Monday night, when they'd officially lived together for a week. They were sitting on the couch as usual, *Quantum of Solace* playing on the sixty-five-inch screen, when he noticed how far away Taylor was. They were on opposite ends of the sofa, not even close enough for an accidental casual touch, let alone something purposeful.

He hadn't touched Taylor since the first weekend Taylor had slept over.

He remembered the warmth and weight of Taylor's head on his thigh, the sensation of Taylor's hair between his fingers, the feel of company and closeness. He missed it.

Did Taylor?

"Do you...?" His voice trailed off, but when Taylor looked at him, he pushed to finish his sentence. How the hell did he ask? "Do you want to put your head in my lap?" That sounded like a terrible come-on.

Taylor looked surprised. "Can I?" There was an eagerness in his voice that soothed Harold's embarrassment.

"Of course." He patted his leg. "Here, boy."

Taylor grinned, his face lighting up, before he bounded over to Harold like an eager puppy. He lay down and snuggled into position. The changing scenes from the TV reflected on Taylor's face in flickers like firelight. He was so handsome. Harold ran his fingers through Taylor's hair, and the soft strands curled around his fingers as if they wanted to keep him. He'd let them if it meant more evenings like this.

The sound of an explosion caught his attention, but as he returned his focus to the screen, he kept petting Taylor. This was what he'd been missing. This felt right.

Chapter Six

Taylor loved lying on the couch while Harold petted him. They'd done it every night since Harold had asked. It was a luxury, and Taylor basked in it, but unlike that first night, the simple attention alone no longer satisfied his urge to play. He wanted more.

Harold had been fine with the scene Taylor had described. Would he freak out if Taylor asked for something different? He was too chicken to ask with words. So on Thursday when Harold was cooking dinner, Taylor went to his knees and crawled to the kitchen doorway. He sat back on his heels and silently watched Harold work. The smells coming from the stove were delicious, and his mouth watered in anticipation.

Maybe this could be enough. If he was quiet, Harold would never know he was there, and he could indulge without having to risk rejection. It wasn't what he wanted, but it was better than nothing, right?

"Just make sure I don't trip over you while I'm moving around the kitchen," Harold said. "If I break my neck, there will be no scraps or treats in the future."

Taylor froze. He'd been so lost in his thoughts he hadn't known he'd been caught. And instead of asking what the hell he was doing, Harold had scolded him like he probably had Missy. His heart raced, and he had to struggle not to bark with joy. He crawled across the floor and nudged Harold's leg with the side of his head in gratitude. Harold reached down to scritch his hair before returning to his cooking. It only made the moment more perfect. Taylor sat back to watch, this time right at his Master's side.

It wasn't long before the enticing smells became too much to resist, and Taylor whined. When Harold looked down at him, he gazed up with his most pitiful pleading expression. To his delight, Harold gave a resigned sigh and held a piece of chicken on a fork down to him.

"Careful, it's hot."

Taylor smiled and chomped the piece of chicken. It seared his tongue and he yelped.

"I warned you," Harold said.

Taylor ignored him as he attempted to chew the piece small enough to swallow without actually touching the delicate parts of his mouth. It was a challenge.

"Are you all right?" Harold asked.

Once the chicken was gone, he was fine. He bumped Harold's leg again to say so. After giving him a quick pet, Harold continued cooking. Taylor refrained from begging for any more scraps.

Eventually, he became bored and left the kitchen. There wasn't much for a pup to do in Harold's apartment. If only there was a ball he could roll or a bed he could snuggle on. He wandered into Harold's bedroom, wondering if there was anything more interesting in there.

The room was carpeted, unlike the rest of the apartment, which had wooden floors that were harsh on Taylor's knees. Harold's closet had sliding doors. He nosed one open and found a pair of shoes set neatly on the floor in front of him. He considered playing with them, but he didn't know if Harold would scold him for it. Moving to the bed, he pawed at Harold's comforter. It was thick and fluffy, tempting Taylor to curl up for a nap. He put his front paws up on the night table to see what Harold kept next to his bed. An alarm clock, a lamp, and a mystery novel. The other night table had a lamp but was otherwise empty. Taylor tried opening one of the drawers with his teeth, but it wouldn't budge, so he abandoned his quest and returned to the kitchen.

I wonder how long until dinner's ready. He reared up to find out.

"Down," Harold scolded sharply. Taylor returned his front paws to the floor. "Almost done, pup. Just a few more minutes."

They'd been eating their dinners on the couch while watching TV, so Taylor bounded back into the living room and settled expectantly next to the coffee table. It wasn't long before Harold emerged from the kitchen carrying two bowls and spoons. He set them on the table where Taylor could see they contained chicken fried rice. Harold sat in his usual spot on the couch and picked up his bowl and one of the spoons. He raised a mouthful to eat, paused, and looked at Taylor.

Was the scene over? No, that was an unfair question. Taylor had started without telling Harold or even asking him. It was unfair to put expectations on him without permission. Regretfully, Taylor pulled himself up onto the couch and sat like a human being. It felt weird.

"Did you want to eat from a bowl on the floor?" Harold asked.

It took a moment for Taylor to find his voice, but Harold waited. Finally, he said, "This bowl is too deep for me to eat everything without using my hands or making a mess. I wouldn't want to risk your rug getting dirty."

Harold rolled his eyes. "You do recall I used to have a dog, right? This rug has seen its fair share of messes."

Yes, Taylor remembered Missy. Terrible as it was, he was jealous of her. Harold had loved her, taken care of her, been her Master. Taylor was the furthest thing from Harold's pet.

"Was that the only reason?" Harold asked.

Taylor bit his lip.

"You can tell me. I know this is something you want, and unless what you have in mind involves a pooper scooper, I think I can handle it."

"That's not one of my kinks," Taylor said.

"But eating out of a dog bowl appeals to you."

Taylor nodded.

"Words, pup. I want words."

The order flooded Taylor with want, and need, and *yes*. "Yes. Sir. I would like to eat out of a dog bowl sometimes. Sir."

"Good boy. Now eat up. There's a new horror movie on Netflix that I've been dying to see."

That's it? Harold's easy acceptance was baffling, but it eased the nervousness Taylor had been battling to answer his questions. "What kind of horror movie?" he asked.

"The over-the-top ridiculous kind."

Taylor smiled. "That's my favorite."

Two days later, Harold was grocery shopping when his conversation with Taylor came back to him. The whole scene in the kitchen came back to him. When he'd noticed Taylor kneeling in the doorway he'd immediately thought of Missy. She'd always watched him cook, hoping some scraps would fall on the floor. Sometimes he'd indulged her.

Caught up with his memories, he'd said the same thing to Taylor he used to say to her. It'd been embarrassing, but Taylor had knelt beside him and gazed up at him with a pleading expression that could have put Missy's to shame. Harold had been a sucker for Missy's begging. It was the same for Taylor's. Whoever said the owner was in charge of the pets had much stronger willpower than him.

It had seemed so natural to offer chicken to Taylor, to warn him as he would have Missy, even to scold him when he'd leaned on the counter. Wasn't that weird, though? If Taylor had been standing, it would have been perfectly reasonable for him to look at the counter or even lean against it, but Taylor's actions had been so doglike that he'd reacted accordingly. And Taylor had gone with it.

He'd even admitted he wanted to eat out of a dog bowl, Harold thought as he eyed the pet aisle. He turned down it and perused the section for dogs. Most of it was food and toys, but at the end he found a small selection of bowls. He put two blueish-gray ones into his basket.

Before moving on, he also grabbed a black squeaky ball. He felt like an idiot, but Missy had loved playing ball. Maybe Taylor would too. Before his embarrassment could get the better of him, he moved on to the next aisle. He succeeded in ignoring his unease until he came home and started unpacking his shopping bags.

"Let me help," Taylor said as he entered the kitchen.

Without thinking, Harold handed him one of the bags.

He was in the middle of putting the milk away when he heard Taylor ask, "What's this?" He turned back to see Taylor holding up the ball. Taylor gave it a squeeze. The high-pitched squeak made his eyes light up. "Is this...?"

"If it's dumb, I'll return it."

"You bought me a toy."

"I can return it."

"You bought me a toy!" Taylor exclaimed and threw his arms around him. "Thank you!"

"So, it wasn't a stupid idea?"

"Are you kidding? This is amazing. Thank you." Taylor gave him a peck on the cheek. Flustered by the show of affection and wondering if he could get some more, Harold said, "I bought you bowls too."

Taylor's grin grew wider, and he pawed through the bags until he pulled out the bowls in question.

"Is the color okay?" Harold asked.

"I want my name on them," Taylor said.

"We can paint it on."

Taylor looked at him, his eyes shining brightly. Harold had never seen anyone so happy, and over a couple of bowls. "They're perfect."

They went back to unpacking, Harold feeling strangely pleased with himself and no longer embarrassed. "Would you want to use them tonight? I can make something easy to eat without your hands."

"You really don't mind?"

"I bought the bowls, didn't I?"

"You did." Taylor's voice was soft. "I've never had pup bowls of my own before."

Harold finished putting the cereal away and turned to him. "Really?"

Taylor nodded. "I've always played casually, usually at

a party or something."

"What about your boyfriends?" *What about Liam?*

"Some of them played with me, but they'd use a plate or one of the flatter bowls we already had if they were feeding me."

None of them had bought a bowl for him? Had Harold gone too far? "What about toys?"

"We had some of those. A ball, usually. I had a rope once and a couple of other things."

"So the ball was a good idea?"

The grin returned. "I can't wait to play with it."

"Dinner first," Harold said. "Come on, let's finish putting this stuff away so I can cook."

He decided to make breaded pork chops. They'd be easy to cut into bite-sized pieces for Taylor to eat. It was unusual, cooking with that thought in mind, but he didn't find it weird. For a side dish, he sautéed string beans and rice. He had no idea how Taylor would eat it, but they'd figure it out.

When it came time to serve, he plated the food in separate piles in Taylor's bowl and set it down next to the coffee table. Taylor, who'd been waiting patiently at his side while he cooked, gave an amused quirk of his lip when he saw it.

"That all right?"

In answer, Taylor bent forward and began eating. Once he was sure Taylor could reach everything, Harold did the same.

Taylor went so far as to lick the bowl when he was done. He finished with a grin, a few stray grains of rice stuck to his face.

"Come here, you." Harold beckoned, patting the seat beside him.

With a bark, Taylor hopped up onto the couch and

settled on his haunches where indicated. Harold grabbed a napkin and wiped his face. "Keep still," he ordered when Taylor squirmed in protest. "Be a good boy or you won't get any ball time."

Taylor stilled and let Harold clean him.

"All right. You're all clean. Go play."

Taylor eagerly descended from the couch and scampered over to where they'd left the ball on the floor. He nuzzled it with his nose, making it roll, and then chased after it. He tried biting it, but it was too big for his mouth. Frustrated, he tried again. And again. On the fourth try, he pushed hard enough to make the ball squeak. It startled him into jumping back, and Harold laughed.

"Bring it here, boy."

Taylor nudged the ball in Harold's direction until it bumped against his toes. Harold picked it up and chucked it lightly across the room. Taylor barked as he chased after it, looking like a happy puppy.

But not quite.

Harold stood and walked to the corner where Taylor kept his stuff. Normally he wouldn't search another person's belongings without permission, but he knew where to find what he was looking for.

Carefully placed in the top of one of Taylor's bags was the mask. He lifted it out and looked at it. It was a full hood in black with gray ears and gray on the sides of the muzzle. There were holes for the eyes and near the chin, probably allowing for Taylor to eat when wearing it. It was softer than he'd expected. He'd thought it would be leather, but it wasn't.

Taylor had quieted while Harold examined the mask. He turned to find Taylor watching him, his expression unreadable. He didn't look as joyful as before.

"Come here, boy," Harold said.

Taylor cautiously crawled to him and sat back on his feet.

"Shall we put this on you?" Harold asked.

Taylor's eyes widened. His lips parted as if he were going to speak, but he didn't.

"You'd like that, wouldn't you? Having your mask while you play?"

Taylor nodded eagerly.

Harold found the snaps to open the hood and maneuvered it over Taylor's head. It was an uncoordinated process, but they succeeded in the end. Once it was closed, Taylor let out another bark. Harold patted his head. "Go and play."

Taylor did as bid, pushing the ball around with his now-canine nose. Harold went back to the couch to watch. Occasionally, Taylor nudged the ball over to him, and Harold threw it. They played for a while until Taylor flopped down onto the couch, his head landing in its usual place on Harold's lap. He looked worn out but happy.

"We might have to get another one of these," Harold said as he ran his fingers over the fabric on the back of Taylor's head. "I like it when I can pet your hair."

Taylor prodded his hand, tilting his head to bring his cheek, and the snaps, closer to Harold's fingers.

"You want me to take it off?"

Taylor did it again.

Harold carefully unclasped the mask and slipped it off. He ran his fingers through Taylor's hair. It was damp with sweat but still soft.

"You worked really hard today, didn't you, boy?"

Taylor nestled into his thigh and closed his eyes.

"Yeah, just relax now. You did really good." Harold

turned on the TV using the remote app on his phone. He put on a movie but didn't pay attention to what it was. Instead, he watched his pup drifting off to sleep while he petted him.

During his nap, Taylor reached down a couple of times to rub his knee. Curious, Harold gently lifted the younger man's pant leg until he could see the joint. It was an angry red. He hadn't thought about what the hard wood of his floor would do to Taylor's knees. Even the rug he owned wasn't thick enough cushioning for the rambunctious play Taylor had engaged in. Harold would have to invest in kneepads. He wouldn't have Taylor hurting himself.

He considered getting ice for Taylor's knees but that would require dislodging him, and Harold didn't have the heart to do that. Instead, he soothed the skin with his thumb and watched Taylor's sleeping face.

Sometime later Taylor turned over, giving Harold access to his other knee. He carefully shifted the pant leg up and repeated his ministrations on the other leg.

He hadn't thought anything of it, but when Taylor snuggled, Harold suddenly became aware of how close Taylor's face was to his crotch. Taylor's lips parted on a sigh and hot breath ghosted over his pants, seeping through the fabric to the skin beneath. He swallowed as arousal shot through him like a lightning bolt. He needed to extricate himself from this situation before his erection filled the remaining space between them.

"Taylor?" he called softly. "It's time for bed." He smoothed a few stray hairs back from Taylor's forehead. "Taylor?"

Taylor nuzzled in again, and Harold clenched his teeth. He longed to discover what Taylor's mouth would feel like around his cock, but not while the boy was unconscious.

Another breath came, the wet warmth torturously enticing. "Taylor, please wake up."

Slowly, Taylor's eyes opened. He blinked drowsily, then swallowed.

"It's time for bed, Taylor," Harold said.

Taylor rolled his eyes up to look at him.

"You have to let me up."

As if in a daze, Taylor wriggled down until his head was no longer on Harold's lap. Harold stood, allowing him to straighten out again.

"Are you going to sleep like that?"

Taylor snuggled in more tightly on the couch, and Harold took that as an affirmative. He grabbed Taylor's pillow and guided it under his head, then covered him with the blanket from the other end of the couch.

"Have a good night," he said, placing a kiss on Taylor's forehead before he could think better of it.

After escaping to his room and shutting the door behind him, he palmed his aching cock. He could still feel the ghostly touch of Taylor's breath, the weight of his head, and the sight of those thin lips. He squeezed, letting the sharp bite of pain abate his need while he changed. Under the covers he took himself in hand again and let his imagination run freely.

He pictured Taylor lying peacefully on his lap like before, face inches from his zipper. Instead of backing away from the temptation, Harold let it build, his desire growing stronger and harder between them. In his mind he called to Taylor, and Taylor's eyes drifted open. He saw the unmistakable evidence of Harold's erection and looked up.

There was a moment where Harold's fantasy paused, caught on a precipice as he decided which way to go with it. In the privacy of his bedroom, he felt daring. He slid his hand into Taylor's hair, cupping the back of his head and tugging. Harold could almost feel the silky strands between his fingers.

Taylor boldly responded to his...request? Inquiry? Permission? Whatever it was, he extended his chin and blew hot air purposefully over Harold's cock. He rubbed his nose against it and whimpered. Unable to wait any longer, Harold shoved Taylor's face into his groin. Taylor went willingly, pressing his face even closer and rubbing his cheek against the hard rod encased in denim.

"You want it?" Harold growled.

Taylor nodded with a whine.

"Then take it."

With a finesse only possible in dreams, Taylor unbuttoned Harold's pants and drew the zipper down with his teeth. Like magic, Harold's erection sprang free, the underwear he usually wore vanishing with the whim of his fantasy. Taylor nuzzled close again, strands of his hair tickling Harold's skin and getting caught in the drops of pre-cum Harold was using to slick his dick in real life. In the daydream, Taylor licked his cock, but the illusion was moving too slowly. Harold was going to spend soon.

"Take it now, boy," he said, unaware if he was speaking out loud or only in his imagination.

Fantasy Taylor pressed his head back against Harold's hand, and by the rules of make-believe, Harold knew he wanted to be controlled instead of released. Harold guided his erection into Taylor's mouth and pulled his head forward. The urgency of reality's deadline forced his hand,

and in his mind, Harold used Taylor fast and hard. The boy took it all eagerly. He ended by shoving himself deep into Taylor's throat as he spent both in his dream and in truth.

His seed hot on his hand and belly, Harold couldn't remember the last time he'd come that hard.

Chapter Seven

The following morning was Sunday. Harold loved lazy Sunday mornings. He stretched, content to remain in his cocoon of blankets for a while longer. The bed was warm and comfortable, and he had nowhere he needed to be.

Rubbing a hand along his stomach, he reached for his morning wood and gave it a tug. The smell of sex still lingered after his hasty cleanup last night, reminding him of his fantasy and the intense orgasm it had given him. He snaked a hand inside his pants, relishing the direct contact on his skin, and stroked languidly. Sunday mornings really were the best.

A shifting of weight on his mattress caught his attention, and he froze. Cracking one eye open, he saw a lump at the foot of his bed. It was a mound of brown fuzzy blanket, the version both he and Taylor owned. Since it was the wrong color to be his, he had to assume it was Taylor's and therefore Taylor must be beneath it.

What was Taylor doing at the foot of his bed?

Harold carefully removed his hand from his pants. It was a good thing he'd noticed before he'd gone any further with his indulgence. It was bad enough he'd used Taylor as spank bank material. To masturbate while the man in question lay next to his feet was another level altogether.

"Good morning, Taylor."

The bundle of blanket shifted until a head with tousled brown hair popped out.

"Are you speaking this morning?"

Taylor nodded but no words emerged. Finally, a croaky "Thirsty" came out.

Harold always brought a bottle of water into his bedroom when he went to sleep for precisely this kind of moment. He handed the bottle to Taylor. Taylor snaked a hand out from beneath the covers, took it, and drank in long swigs.

"Dare I ask how you ended up in here?" Harold asked.

"I crawled."

That gave Harold a moment's pause as he pictured Taylor crawling across the floor from the living room to the bedroom, his muscles sliding beneath the bare skin of his back.

As hot as that thought was, he asked, "Any reason why?"

How the hell could Taylor answer that? A part of him had just wanted to be close. That had been the motivation of his inner pup, seeking the comfort and safety he'd received when he lay on Harold's lap. The other part of him...

Last night he'd woken disoriented to find himself alone on the couch. He'd vaguely remembered Harold leaving. He'd gotten up to relieve himself and change when he'd heard noise coming from Harold's room.

"Take it now, boy."

The words had halted his steps, and the unmistakable sounds of sex—or in this case, masturbation—that had followed had made it impossible for Taylor to turn away. Instead, he'd moved closer to the door, straining to listen. It hadn't been long before Harold had finished, and the sound of him coming had sent Taylor to his knees in the hall. He'd had to cover his mouth not to cry out.

He'd knelt there unmoving until he'd heard Harold rise from the bed. Before he could be caught, he'd scrambled on shaky legs into the bathroom and shut the door behind him. Safely alone, he'd thrust his hand into his sweats and beat one out, coming quicker than he'd thought possible.

After cleaning up, changing, and checking the coast was clear, he'd flopped back onto the couch without bothering to open it. The sound of Harold's orgasm had echoed in his mind, filling him with a yearning to be closer. He'd fallen asleep horny and lonely and dreamed he'd crawled into his Master's bed. Apparently, it hadn't been a dream.

He wasn't telling any of that to Harold, though. The man had been shy enough handling his morning wood in front of Taylor. What would he think if he knew Taylor had eavesdropped on his performance last night?

Taylor shrugged.

Harold sighed. "There is a thing called privacy, you know. And permission."

"You can punish me for not having permission. As for privacy, would you have cared if Missy were here?"

"Yes."

The answer came quick enough it could have been a lie. Taylor quirked a brow.

"Maybe. I don't know. I probably would have kicked her off the bed."

"Doesn't mean she'd leave the room," Taylor pointed out.

"What does that have to do with anything?"

"You can act as if I were a real dog," Taylor said. He couldn't help adding with a smirk, "Perhaps I can be better than a real dog."

Harold's face flushed, the color tinting his cheekbones above his beard. Taylor wondered what had been in his fantasy last night to make him react like that.

"It's time to get up," Harold said.

Taylor let him change the subject and rose from the bed. "Do we have plans for today?"

"I'm free. What about you?"

"Free as a bird."

"We could take a walk," Harold suggested. "It's a nice day out."

"A walk in the park?" Taylor asked. "Will you play fetch with me?"

"Hmm," Harold mused. "I may have a Frisbee somewhere we can use."

"Are you serious?"

"Depends. Can you catch a Frisbee in your mouth?"

"Unfortunately, I'm not that skilled."

"Pity, that would have been impressive. Now I'm not sure I want to play."

Taylor pouted. "We can still play, can't we?" He widened his eyes and tried to look pitiful.

"You're wasting your talents. I wasn't going to say no."

"Even natural talents need refinement through practice."

"Be careful or I'll become immune."

"Impossible," Taylor said. "There's no cure for being a sucker for animals."

"You aren't an animal, you know."

"Technically…"

Harold sighed. "Go make us some coffee. I'm going to see if I can find the Frisbee."

Taylor felt buoyant as he went into the kitchen. He constantly marveled at how much Harold was willing to indulge him. He didn't need to be a pup all the time—he didn't want to be—but in a way he'd done more pup play with Harold than with anyone else.

In the past, his opportunities for play had been scheduled scenes or at a party. Each instance had had its structure dictated by time, location, and checklists. This was more casual. The play was lighter, but the atmosphere made up for it. He felt more relaxed with Harold than with any other Master he'd been with.

He hadn't realized he'd wanted something like this, something where pup play could be part of his everyday life, in little things and done spontaneously. He didn't have to wait for that next party opportunity or schedule a scene ahead of time. It could just happen.

Perhaps he was making more of this than there was. He'd felt deprived of his kink for a while, as if he'd been begging for scraps wherever he could find them. It was part of the reason he and Liam hadn't worked out. Liam was kinky, but he wasn't into service at all. He didn't care for play parties, and although he was a switch, he preferred to sub. That didn't work for Taylor, whose biggest kink was being a pup.

Taylor's cell rang at the same time the electric kettle beeped to tell him the water had boiled. He ran to grab his phone and answered it as he poured water into two mugs of instant coffee.

"Hello?"

"Why did you lie to me?" The sound of Liam's voice almost made Taylor miss the mug and pour boiling water on his hand.

"What are you talking about?"

"I know you're not staying at Joanne's."

"Stalking me much?"

"Her new contract is with Melissa."

Oh. Melissa was one of their acquaintances from the BDSM community. She and Liam had gotten on like a house on fire and were really close. She'd totally tell him if she'd agreed to a contract with Joanne. Taylor sighed. "I didn't want to fight."

"What is there to fight about?" Liam asked.

"I'm staying with a guy. I didn't want you to get upset about it."

"Ah." Taylor knew he'd hurt him. Liam didn't speak in one-word replies unless he was hiding his emotions. "Anyone I know?"

"No, he's a new acquaintance, but he's been kind enough to let me stay until our lease is up."

Taylor flinched as Harold entered the kitchen. Had he heard Taylor call him an acquaintance? The thought made him feel guilty. As did being on the phone with Liam while they were supposed to be spending time together. He handed Harold one of the mugs as an apology.

"Are you moving in with him?" Liam asked.

"No, it's temporary." He wasn't going to impose on Harold longer than he had to. The man had been kind enough to let him stay this long.

"What are you going to do after the lease is over?"

"Move somewhere else," Taylor said.

"Have you found a place?"

"Not yet, but I'm working on it." At least, he would be after this phone call was over.

"I don't want to live alone," Liam said.

"I don't think either of us could afford to," Taylor replied, but he understood that wasn't what Liam had meant. "You can find a roommate to share with. Wasn't one of your buddies from the salon looking for a place? Why don't you share with him?"

"You mean Peter? He's a slob. I'd go crazy in three days."

"So not him, but I'm sure you'll be able to find someone. Ask around."

Liam sighed. "Yeah, I know. I just..."

"Don't like change."

"Yeah." Taylor could hear the wry smile in his voice.

"Look, I've got to go. I'll call and check in later, okay? See how you're doing? We also need to find a time to go over that bookcase. There's no way I'm letting you leave with what's mine."

"You mean you're going to try to steal what's mine," Liam retorted, his amusement genuine and familiar.

"Damn straight."

Liam laughed.

They were both in a better mood when they hung up, and the reminder that Taylor was going for a walk with Harold made Taylor's earlier excitement return in full force. He was smiling as he left the kitchen.

Harold was sitting on the couch with his laptop. He didn't look as thrilled about their walk as Taylor was.

"Are you okay?" Taylor asked.

Harold closed the computer's lid and set it on the coffee table. "Sure. Fine."

He didn't sound fine. Hopefully the walk would fix that. "Ready to go?"

"Yeah."

Taylor didn't push. They grabbed light jackets and the Frisbee and headed out.

It was the perfect day for a walk. Fluffy clouds sparsely dotted the blue spring sky like a postcard picture stating *Wish you were here*. The breeze was warm and occasionally perfumed with the scent of flowers when it wasn't polluted with the stench of the sewer or garbage.

Despite the lovely atmosphere, Harold's mood hadn't improved. "Are we on a date?" Taylor asked, hoping to shake him out of it.

"What?"

"Is this a date?"

"I thought we were going to the park to play fetch."

"Couldn't we do both?"

Harold tilted his head thoughtfully. He already looked happier as they chatted. "I don't know, can you?"

Ah. "I'm not gonna go all out. I wouldn't in a public place."

"You do at those parties you've mentioned."

"Those are safe spaces, not *public* places."

"Hmm," Harold said. "So, does this trip to the park do anything for you if you can't let go like you can at home?"

Home. That was a lovely word, especially when linked to his ability to play there. "Going on a date with a hot Daddy definitely does something for me."

"We haven't established that this is a date yet, and wait, what do you mean Daddy?"

"That's what Joanne thinks of you as. Are you into women?"

"No. And I'm definitely not into age play or whatever they call it."

"That's good. I wouldn't want her getting any ideas she can steal you from me."

"I wasn't aware I was yours to steal."

Taylor felt his face go hot. Had he been thinking of Harold that way? Yes. Yes, he had. "Well, right now you are because we're on a date."

"Are we now?"

"Yes. Because I say so. And we're going to go play fetch, get a nice dinner, and then you're gonna take me to a movie or out dancing or something because that's what happens on dates."

Harold had never been on a date where playing fetch was part of the itinerary, but Taylor was unlike any of the guys he'd dated before. That was good because most of the men he'd dated had been shits, or as Madeline would have it, bores. If the young man who looked like he'd stepped off the page of a porn magazine wanted him to take him out on a date, Harold would have to be shot before he said no. And probably not even then.

You should say no, his logical brain prompted. *He's moving out soon. He said so not twenty minutes ago.*

Yeah, Taylor had said that right when Harold had been scouring the internet for kneepads and wondering what else the pup could use as he scampered around the living room. As soon as the words "acquaintance" and "move somewhere else" hit the air, a sour churning had filled his gut. What was he doing buying stuff for a guest who would be gone in a matter of weeks?

And yet, Taylor had given him more comfort and companionship in a matter of days than all his previous boyfriends combined.

"Well?" Taylor asked. He'd stepped up close, blocking Harold's way so Harold had to stop short to keep from bowling him over. His beautiful face was easily accessible for kissing and was oh-so-tempting, just like the rest of him. Taylor didn't need puppy dog eyes for Harold to want to give him anything he asked for. Harold wanted to do that anyway.

"Yes," Harold said. "We're going on a date."

And he was going to buy those kneepads as soon as they got back home.

Chapter Eight

The park was full of pedestrians taking advantage of the nice weather. They managed to find an area big enough to throw the Frisbee around without risking their neighbors, and it wasn't long before a group of children asked to join in the fun. They ended up in a big circle where someone would call out a name before throwing the disk to that person. By the time they decided to take a break, it was well past lunchtime.

"Food?" Harold asked.

"Food," Taylor confirmed with a nod.

They headed toward the edge of the park but hadn't gone far when someone called out "Taylor?" Harold cringed, hoping they hadn't bumped into Taylor's ex. Taylor brightened at the sound of the voice.

They turned to see a handsome man in a wheelchair. He looked about Harold's age, though his skin was more weathered. He'd probably spent a lot of time outdoors whereas Harold was a homebody usually sequestered in front of a computer. The man was muscular as well. Harold could imagine him lifting weights or doing heavy labor.

Ice blue eyes fixed on him, and Harold started, feeling guilty for staring. "Sorry," he offered as an apology for his rudeness.

"James!" Taylor exclaimed with a grin. "What are you doing here?"

"Going for a walk. Like you."

"We didn't just walk," Taylor said, his chin lifting smugly.

"Oh?"

"We played Frisbee."

James laughed. "You always find joy in the little things."

"It isn't little," Taylor protested.

"You're right," James said. "My apologies. And who is this?" He nodded toward Harold.

That was a good question. Harold wanted to know who James was as well.

"This is Harold. He's letting me stay with him for a while and indulging me in...little things."

"I thought we established they aren't little?"

Taylor smiled.

James turned to Harold. "I haven't seen you at community events. Do you only play privately?"

At first Harold didn't understand what James was referring to. When he did, a thousand questions rose up in him at once. Were the "community events" he spoke of the parties Taylor went to? Did that mean he'd played with Taylor? What had they done? Had they had sex?

"This is my first time playing," Harold said, feeling awkward with his response. He'd never been one to talk about his personal life to strangers. Even though he and Taylor hadn't had sex, what they'd done felt just as personal.

James's eyebrows rose in surprise. "Really? Were you

familiar before you met Taylor or has he been your complete introduction?"

What was it to him?

"He's new, but really good," Taylor said. "He has a natural instinct for it."

"I'm glad to hear that, but everyone can use a little guidance no matter how good they are naturally."

Before Harold could inquire what he meant by that, a young man bounded up to them, panting.

"There you are, James! I told you not to leave without me." The newcomer was tall and thin with limpid brown eyes and an untamed mess of black curls.

"I haven't gone far. I knew you'd find me."

"That's not the point," the boy huffed.

"You remember Taylor, don't you, Ezra?" James asked, gesturing toward Taylor.

"Oh!" Ezra exclaimed. "Hi, Taylor. It's good to see you." The smile the boy gave could light up a room. Maybe it wasn't James who'd played with Taylor before.

"Good to see you too. How are things?"

Ezra grinned. "I moved in on Thursday."

"You?" Taylor pointed a finger back and forth between them. "You're living together now?" He looked at James. "You're living with someone?"

"Crazy as the idea is, I find no reason to keep my solitary existence any longer. Ezra has seen me at my worst, and if he can put up with that, I am not letting him go anywhere."

Ezra looked down at James, clear affection in his gaze. Witnessing the connection between them eased the tension in Harold's shoulders.

"Who's the hot Daddy?" Ezra asked.

"That's the second time I've been called that today," Harold muttered.

"Only the second?"

"This is Harold," Taylor said. "He's been letting me stay with him until I find a new place. And he's not a Daddy. He's a Master."

Well, that was new.

"Yours?" Ezra asked.

Taylor nodded.

"It's like we don't even need to be here for this conversation," James said to Harold.

Harold laughed, more of the tension easing from his muscles. "What did you mean by everyone could use some guidance?"

James rolled closer so they could talk more privately. Taylor and Ezra were happily chatting away without them.

"How much do you know about the kink lifestyle?" James asked.

"Only what I've gathered from Taylor and the little research I've done online."

"You must have questions. Ones it would be easier for a person to answer than a computer."

"I'm fond of computers," Harold said. "They're my livelihood."

"A programmer?" At Harold's nod, James said, "I'll keep that in mind. I could use a programmer."

"I'm not cheap."

"Nothing good ever is."

"James," Ezra called. "We're going to be late, and you know Olivia will kill us if we're late."

James sighed. "He's right, I'm afraid." He reached into a pocket and held out a business card. "Feel free to get in touch. I'd be happy to answer those questions.

At the very least, please give me your contact information. I wasn't kidding when I said I needed a programmer."

Harold took the card. He wasn't sure about the kink guidance, but work was work. "I'll be in touch."

James and Ezra said goodbye and headed off.

"We were on our way to get food, weren't we?" Harold asked.

"I'm glad you remembered. I'm starving."

"Mario's?"

"We order from them all the time," Taylor whined. "This is a date, Harold. Take me somewhere nice."

"Wasn't it only minutes ago you were referring to me as Master? How come you're the one who's bossy?"

"That was for when we're playing. Right now, I'm not a pup, I'm potential boyfriend material, and you're taking me out on a date."

"Whoa, whoa, whoa. Slow down there. I agreed to a date. No one said anything about boyfriends. That's quite a jump from date one."

"You don't think I'm boyfriend material?" Taylor asked, looking at him with those fucking puppy dog eyes.

"You're a little shit, that's what you are," Harold said, his heart melting. "Come on, I'll take you to Fenicottero."

"Wow, pulling out the big guns."

"The big guns require a dress code. This is standard grade A first date."

"So, I should look forward to the dress code on our anniversary?"

"Let's see if you make it through date one before we start renting any tuxes."

"Whoa, whoa, whoa," Taylor said, obviously mimicking his earlier exclamation. "Dress codes mean suits or slacks and a nice shirt. Tuxes are for weddings. Now who's rushing things?"

"Shut up."

Taylor grinned. "You didn't disagree."

"You're a brat."

"Yup," Taylor said smugly.

Harold reached out to playfully push his head but ended up stroking his hair and pulling him closer instead. *This six-week limit is going to kill me*, he thought as he slid an arm around Taylor's shoulders. *I'm already done for.*

They were seated in a booth at the back of the restaurant. Harold would have liked to people watch out the window, but this was nicer for a date atmosphere. It was like they were alone in their own corner of the universe.

They perused the menus and ordered, then tucked into the basket of warm bread that had been left for them.

"It's *garlic*." Taylor moaned in a manner that was utterly inappropriate for a dinner table.

When Harold took a bite, he couldn't help letting out a moan of his own. The bread had just the right amount of butter and a perfect amount of seasoning. The garlic was fresh too, as was the parsley.

"This is delicious," he said. He'd eat the whole basket if he wasn't careful.

"Orgasmic."

"I got that impression from the noises you were making."

"I wasn't the only one making them."

"Maybe we should tone it down," Harold said. "There are other people in the restaurant."

"If they're put off by our noises and not making any of their own, their taste buds are dead."

"Be that as it may, they are the majority, and I don't want our date ruined by the Orgasmic Food Police."

"Orgasmic Food Police?"

"Yes. They'll mob us, take away all our good food, and send us home with only packets of ramen for the next month."

"Hey, I like ramen."

"Would you rather have ramen than the dinner we ordered?"

"Point taken." Taylor gasped. "We should go for ramen on our second date. Good ramen. I know a few places."

"Good ramen? There is such a thing?"

Taylor's eyes were so wide Harold thought they might fall out. "You've never had real ramen? Like the kind that doesn't come in a square plastic bag or a paper bowl?"

"Uh, no, I haven't."

"We are fixing that, pronto. Forget our second date. We're doing that tomorrow for lunch."

"Tomorrow is Monday. You'll be at your office during lunch."

"Dinner then. The first opportunity! We're going to fix this."

"I didn't realize there was anything to fix."

"That's because you don't know any better." Taylor reached across the table and patted Harold's hand. "Don't worry, I'll teach you. It'll be my treat. I never did buy you dinner for letting me stay with you."

Harold hadn't planned on holding Taylor to that offer, but he'd agreed at the time, and he couldn't refuse now. "Okay." After popping another piece of orgasmic bread in his mouth, savoring it, and swallowing, he asked, "How do you know James?"

Taylor sat back in his chair, setting his hands in his lap. Harold missed their warmth.

"He's in the community. Though I'm sure you figured that out," Taylor said.

"Have you played with him?"

"Yes."

Harold had figured but didn't like having his theory confirmed. "Pup play?"

Taylor nodded. "It was how I met Ezra. His main kink is pain, but he likes doing the pup thing from time to time."

"What did you do with them?"

Taylor tilted his head. "Do you really want to know?"

Did he? "Yes."

Taylor took a deep breath. "I went to a party with Joanne, and we met Ezra there. I'd gone dressed in my gear hoping to find someone to play with, and Ezra was looking for the same. We decided to do a scene together, and he took me to a private room where James was waiting."

Taylor paused to take a drink of his water. Harold did the same.

"We played together, similar to what I did in the living room last night. We wrestled and chased each other around the room. After a while James threw us a ball and we played with that, batting it around until we were tired. Eventually, Toby and I curled up on the bed next to James."

"Toby?"

"That's Ezra's pup name."

"Do you have a pup name?"

Taylor shook his head. "I've never felt like I needed one. I think in Ezra's case it helps him to get into the headspace. I've never had any trouble doing that."

"I'm aware," Harold teased, and Taylor smiled. "What happened next?"

Taylor's fingers tightened around his glass of water. He seemed nervous to continue. "Toby was turned on, so James gave him a pillow to hump until he came."

A rush of heat flooded Harold. It hit him in the face and pooled down to his groin. He'd heard Taylor's words, but it hadn't been Ezra he'd pictured humping the pillow. It had been Taylor, and the idea had been hot.

He took another sip of water to moisten his suddenly dry mouth. "What about you?"

Taylor shook his head. "Pup play isn't always about sex for me."

"Not always or never?" *Please don't say never.*

Something must have shown on his face because Taylor's nervousness vanished, and a smirk took its place. "If my Master wanted it, then yes."

That wasn't what Harold wanted to hear. "What about what you want?"

Taylor smoothed his expression. "It depends. Sometimes I need to let go, be a puppy, play and escape. Other times..."

Harold was beginning to understand. "Pup play fulfills different needs for you."

Taylor nodded. "Sometimes it is a need. Other times, it's a game and those games could be sexual." The smirk returned. "I did say I could be more useful than a real dog."

He had. Flashes of Harold's fantasy came back to him along with the memory of finding Taylor at the foot of his bed that morning when he'd wanted to take care of another hard-on. The possibilities surged through Harold's mind in a euphoric flood. If the server hadn't shown up at that moment with their food, he might have grabbed Taylor's wrist and dragged him all the way home.

Their date was going excellently. The food was delicious, the company was enjoyable, and Taylor was eighty percent sure Harold was ready to fuck him up against the door as soon as they got home. He couldn't have planned a better day.

Except it didn't happen.

They had a great time. They ate, they chatted, they laughed. They'd been so distracted talking, they forgot to order dessert. Eventually their waiter's inquiries on whether they wanted their check had turned into the check being placed on the table with a few mints, a polite smile, and the not-so-subtle hint to get the hell out so the restaurant could close.

They'd picked up ice cream on their walk home. The night was cool, the sky clear. It was easy to ignore the signs of city grime around them when Taylor had such an engaging companion beside him. Occasionally, their shoulders bumped as they strolled. He wondered if they'd all been on purpose. He knew some of them had since he'd been the one to do it.

Everything had been wonderful, but when they got home, there was no sudden grab and steamy kiss. There wasn't even a simple good night kiss or any kiss at all. After the front door closed, Harold hung up his jacket and headed for the bathroom.

"I'm going to take a shower."

"What?"

"I said I'm going to take a shower."

"I heard you."

"Then why did you ask?"

"Because I'm wondering why you're walking away from

me. Was it my imagination or did we have a great first date?"

"We did."

"So why are you leaving?"

"Date's over, isn't it?"

"No, it isn't! Where's my good night kiss?"

Harold turned to him. Crossing his arms in front of his body, he lifted his shirt up, over his head, and off. His torso was as fit as Taylor had imagined, and his arms were perfect for manhandling. Taylor's body thrummed with the desire to be pressed against a bed by those arms. He swallowed and dragged his gaze up to Harold's face.

"I don't kiss on the first date," Harold said with a smirk that could rival one of Taylor's own. Without another word, he went into the bathroom and shut the door behind him.

What. An. Asshole! How dare he turn the tables on Taylor like that? It wasn't fair! Was Harold punishing him for his own tease earlier? Would he think to do that? Taylor felt his heart melt a little at the idea. Harold really did make a great Master. Thinking of it that way, the denial didn't seem so bad.

No, it totally sucked, but as a punishment Taylor could accept it.

Maybe.

Man, he was horny.

Feeling a little rebellious and still very annoyed, Taylor went into Harold's room and flopped onto the bed. He wriggled, messing up the neatly made sheets in frustration. Crawling forward, he pulled the comforter off the pillows and pressed his face into the downy softness. He could smell Harold in the fabric and groaned. Harold smelled so good. Taylor had seen the bottle of aftershave he used in the bathroom. The name wasn't on the bottle, only a symbol, but the smell was intoxicating.

He breathed in deeper and wriggled more, seeking friction for his growing erection. He'd masturbated a few times to thoughts of Harold. It was an even stronger temptation now, surrounded by his scent and longing for his kiss.

Would Harold punish me if I masturbated on his bed? How would he do it?

Taylor wasn't going to find out. Except he was already reaching down to rub his cock through his jeans. He wouldn't have to get naked or anything. He could hump the bed to get off, and there wouldn't be any trace of what he'd done except for the messed-up bedding, which he'd planned to leave anyway.

Would Harold want to watch him hump the bed? He'd seemed to like the idea when Taylor mentioned Toby doing it. Taylor's hips rocked as he imagined Harold as his audience. Would he want Taylor naked for it?

Taylor pulled Harold's pillow closer, snuggling into it as if the action could extract more of the man's scent. He knew he should leave, but the part of his brain allocated for reason had abandoned him. He stroked his erection again. It was fully hard now, and he pressed it firmly into the mattress as he moved. It wasn't enough. He wanted his clothing gone, but no matter how bratty he felt, that was a line he would not cross without permission. Instead, he alternated humping the mattress with strokes of his hand, lost to the pleasure and need.

"What are you doing?"

Terror shot through Taylor, making him bolt upright. Heat flooded his face and neck when he saw Harold standing in the doorway.

Fuck, I'm in trouble.

Harold was clad in only a towel, beads of water clinging to his shoulders where they'd dripped from his hair and his chest below his beard. He held a second towel against his head. Taylor assumed he'd been drying his hair before he'd caught Taylor in his bed.

So much skin.

Harold's body was in good shape. He went to the gym five days a week to battle the softness that inevitably came from sitting in front of a computer all day, and his efforts had paid off. Taylor highly appreciated the results.

I want to lick every inch of him.

"Is my puppy horny?" Harold asked.

Yes. So horny. Please lose that towel around your waist. Taylor whined.

"So you thought you'd rub one out on my bed?"

Yes. Taylor's hips rocked, missing the friction he'd had moments ago.

"Who said you could do that?"

Is he going to punish me? Excitement rushed through Taylor. He whimpered, pressing low on the bed and rolling his eyes up to look at Harold sorrowfully.

Harold swallowed, and Taylor wondered if he was nervous. *No, please continue. You're doing so well. I need this. I need to come. Please let me come.*

"Good dogs don't get up on the furniture without permission," Harold said. He pointed to the floor. "Down." The growl in his voice shot through Taylor, almost sending him over the edge. He moaned, carefully rising on his hands and knees and crawling off the bed to sit where Harold had pointed. *Please don't stop now. Please let me come.*

"Stay." Harold ordered, and then he left the room.

Taylor panicked for a moment, but he'd been ordered to

stay. That meant Harold was still playing with him. He was coming back, and he'd continue.

He was right. Harold came back with one of the throw pillows from the couch. He tossed it down on the floor in front of Taylor.

"You want to come? Use that."

The order sent a shiver of excitement through Taylor's body. He crawled forward to position the pillow between his legs. It was soft, offering minimal resistance as he rested his groin against it. Getting a decent amount of friction would be a challenge. Had Harold chosen this particular pillow with that in mind? He tried rocking his hips. There was scant sensation gained by the action. Shifting his weight onto his front paws, he spread his legs to get lower and canted his hips forward. That was better.

He could imagine what he looked like with his back arched and his knees spread shamelessly to keep contact with the pillow. He hoped Harold was enjoying the view.

Harold was. Sort of. A part of him was freaking out. He hadn't thought about the denseness of the pillow and if it would work for this. He'd just grabbed the first one he'd seen.

Taylor humped the pillow, falling into a rhythm only to stop with a grunt and shift to a better position. Was he ruining this for Taylor by making him frustrated?

He'd tell me if he didn't like this, right?

Despite his doubts, he had to admit the scene in front of him was *hot*. The struggle only made it more so. Taylor was trying hard to get off and the grunts and groans he made when things weren't working went straight to Harold's cock.

The only thing that would have made it better was if Taylor had been naked or in that G-string he'd been wearing when Harold had found him. Taylor's erection was lost to the fabric of his jeans and the pillow, but Harold could imagine how the tip would peek out, how it would be red, angry, and dripping by now. He wanted to see it. He wanted to see it *badly*.

Taylor needed to finish so Harold could handle his own hard-on. It was aching, and Harold was using all his willpower not to grab it and start jerking off in Taylor's face.

"If you don't come in the next two minutes, you're not coming at all tonight."

He had no idea if Taylor would listen to the restriction. The important part was Taylor needed to come *now*. His pup whimpered and rocked his hips faster. He made needy little sounds as he thrust against the pillow that tore at Harold's withering grasp on his control.

Harold held on as long as he could before he said, "Ten seconds, Taylor." As he counted down, Taylor's desperation grew more apparent. The young man was sweating, and the noises he made grew louder.

"Seven, six, five..."

Taylor was truly like an animal now, rutting with abandon, his knees spread as wide as they could go. His brow was furrowed with determination, lips parted, and each breath emerged as a grunt. It was a magnificent sight to behold.

"Three, two, one, now, pup," Harold ordered.

With a shocking yell, Taylor's body jerked. He stiffened and threw his head back, the column of his neck stretched taut. When he relaxed, Harold could see a wet spot on his jeans.

Oh fuck. I'm going to come. "Out, pup," he ordered. "And take the pillow with you."

As if he knew the last straw to killing all of Harold's reason, Taylor wriggled back to take the pillow in his teeth. He carried it out that way, still on all fours. It was more than Harold could handle. As soon as Taylor was gone, he ripped the towel off his hips and tugged frantically at his erection. In no time at all he was coming, white drops falling onto the carpet at his feet.

Spent, he collapsed on the bed. That was the hottest thing he'd ever seen, and the most nerve-racking. Harold rolled onto his back, waiting for his heart rate to return to normal. He couldn't define why, but something about what he'd just done felt risky. Before, he'd always moved carefully, testing each step into the unknown before setting his weight on it. This had felt like running and taking a giant leap. There was no way he could do that again without knowing more about what he was doing. James had been right. He needed to talk to someone about all this. He made a point to call first thing in the morning.

Until then, he needed to clean up and make sure Taylor was all right with what had happened. He used his towel to do a cursory wipe of the floor, threw on a pair of sweats and a T-shirt, and headed for the living room.

Taylor was lying on the rug, the pillow abandoned beside him. Harold took a seat next to him and ran his fingers gently through the young man's hair.

"Taylor?"

Taylor's eyes fluttered open.

"Are you okay?"

Taylor nodded.

"Are you speaking yet?"

Taylor tilted his hand in a so-so manner.

"I need to know if I did anything wrong."

Taylor gasped and sat up. "What? No. That was amazing. Oh..." He pressed a hand to his head. "Wasn't ready to sit up yet."

Harold pulled him close and made him lean back against his chest. "Sorry."

"It's okay. I have to get up to take a shower anyway before my jeans permanently glue themselves to my body."

"I'm sure you have a minute or two before that happens."

"Yeah," Taylor said with a sigh, settling in against Harold's chest. "This is nice aftercare."

"Aftercare?"

"After a scene you check in with each other to make sure everyone is okay."

"We haven't been doing that, have we?"

"Not in a defined sense, but we usually end up cuddling on the couch, which is pretty much the same."

"What about now?"

"You just asked me how I was, didn't you? And now you're taking care of me."

"Did you like what we did?"

"Hell yes," Taylor said with emphasis. "God, that was hot. That little growl you made when you told me to get off the bed almost made me come. And when you did tell me to come..." He shuddered. "Fuck, that was intense."

"Really?"

Taylor shifted so he could look up at him. "I loved it," he said. "Feel free to use that idea again in the future."

Taylor's enthusiasm had gone a long way to soothe Harold's concern. "I was thinking less clothing next time."

Taylor grinned. "Fuck yes. Yes, please."

Chapter Nine

Harold called James the following morning, and they agreed to meet for lunch. They chose a Greek restaurant ten minutes from Harold's apartment. Despite being close to home, Harold had never been there before. When he walked in, he was greeted with the scent of cooking meat and spices. He inhaled deeply, looking forward to a delicious meal no matter how the conversation went.

"Harold," James called from a table in the far corner. It was distant enough for private conversation, and James's position against the wall allowed him an unobstructed view of the place. "I hope you don't mind; I ordered some spanakopita to start. I'm famished."

"Not at all. Sorry I'm late."

"You're not. I neglected to eat breakfast this morning. Ezra is going to scold me when he finds out." At Harold's curious look, he added, "He's taken it upon himself to make sure I get three square meals a day. There was a time I would forget to eat altogether, and we would both prefer that never happen again."

"I've often forgotten to eat when I'm in the middle of

programming. It would be nice having someone remind me to stop and take a break every once in a while."

James smiled. "It is useful. There were days I lived on alcohol and cigarettes when I was on a job. Being retired does have its silver linings."

"What did you do?"

James waved a hand. "Freelance work. Nothing exciting."

"And now you're retired?" James was young for retirement.

"From that line of work, yes. I'm taking a break while I decide what to do next. Which reminds me, do you do cybersecurity?"

"Sometimes. It's not my favorite, but I don't have a big enough client base to be choosy."

"Are you starved for work?" James asked.

"I wouldn't say starved"—thankfully—"but projects fluctuate, and I'm currently in one of my lulls."

"That means you're free to help with my project. And if things go well, I have contacts I can point your way."

"That would be great. Thank you."

The appetizer arrived. After putting in the rest of their order, they dug in.

"This is delicious," Harold said.

"Yes, their food is spectacular. The closest I've found to actually being in Greece. I make it a point to come here often."

"You've been to Greece?"

"Multiple times," James confirmed. "It is one of my favorite places to get away."

"I went to London years ago, but otherwise I've never been out of the country."

"Why not?" James asked. "You have a portable job. What's keeping you from taking advantage of it?"

"I don't know. I guess I got caught up in the everyday. First, it was establishing myself as a programmer, then it was maintaining a relationship with my boyfriend, and after that there was Missy. I never stopped to change the routine."

"I take it the boyfriend is gone?"

"As is the dog."

"I'm sorry to hear that. About the dog, I mean."

Harold huffed a laugh. "Thank you."

"Now you have a pet who's as portable as the job," James said. "Maybe you should start thinking outside the routine."

"Taylor is already outside my routine," Harold said. "And he's not mine. Not really."

"It didn't seem that way in the park."

"That was our first date."

"And you're already comfortable with each other."

"It's only temporary. I'm letting Taylor crash on my couch until his current lease is up and he can get a place of his own."

"How long will that be?"

"Three more weeks."

"A lot can happen in three weeks."

"Or I could get my hopes up and lose him in the end."

Their waitress appeared with their food, and they paused the conversation while they took their first bites.

"This really is delicious," Harold said.

When they had satisfied the sharper edges of their hunger, James asked, "You won't keep him, but you still Dom for him?"

Harold put his gyro down and looked at him.

"You two are welcome to do as you like," James said, spreading his hands.

"I want to continue."

"But...?"

The conversation had been pleasant so far, but now they'd come to the real reason Harold had called James. "Something happened last night."

"Something that concerns you."

Harold nodded. "Until now, any time Taylor and I have...played, it's felt natural. Sometimes it's a little weird, but I take things slowly and feel my way through."

"And last night?"

"Last night felt...risky. It's never been like that before."

"Risky, how?"

Harold still wasn't comfortable talking about his private life with others, but he needed to talk to someone, and James was his only option. The man was familiar with pup play, with Taylor, and had offered to help him out. Pushing aside his discomfort, he said, "My footing didn't feel as sure. I know Taylor would speak up if I did something he didn't like, but this was the first time I felt it might be a possibility."

"Have you two talked about this?"

"About my being nervous?"

"About what you're doing together."

"Not really. It sort of started on a whim and just continued."

"This is no longer a whim."

James was right about that. "I don't even know what to say."

"Start by asking about last night. He enjoyed it?"

"Yes."

"Ask him what he enjoyed the most. Ask him what else

he might like." James took a sip of his water and asked a question of his own. "Was this pleasure or punishment?"

Harold balked at the word punishment. Then he remembered scolding Taylor for humping his bed, the words he'd used, the orders he'd given.

"Discipline and punishment are a part of pup play," James said. "Some pups are bratty, some not, but they do make mistakes, and like any dog, they need discipline."

"How do you discipline them?"

"Scolding, removing privileges. There are many options. It depends on what works best for the pup. As Taylor's Master you decide if and when to discipline him, as well as how strict the discipline is."

"What do you mean by strict?"

"Discipline in BDSM can be a guiding tool for a submissive. A Dominant will set up rules and structure for the sub, and if the sub breaks those rules, they are punished. The punishment will be something they do not enjoy to prevent them from making the mistake again."

"Our relationship isn't like that," Harold said.

"It doesn't have to be. Like I said, you need to do what works best for you and Taylor, but to do that you need to talk to him about it."

"Is it worth having this conversation if he's going to be gone soon?"

"If you plan on playing with him until then, yes."

Harold sighed. "How do you begin a conversation like this?"

"In my experience, I find the straightforward approach is best."

"Is that what you did with Ezra?" Harold asked, hoping to change the conversation topic from himself.

"When we sat down to talk. Though I suppose you

could say the way we started was also straightforward, if accidental."

"Accidental?"

"I am not fond of being woken up," James said. "I tend to respond... aggressively."

"What happened?"

"I had fallen asleep and was going to miss an appointment. Ezra had no choice but to wake me, and I reacted as expected. We ended up in a position which piqued both of our interests. After straightening out a few details, it turned into a very enjoyable evening. I never did make that appointment."

Harold laughed. "Seems to have worked out for more than an evening."

"Yes." James's smile was fond. "More importantly for this conversation, the morning after, he and I sat down to discuss our interests and limits for going forward."

Harold should have seen that coming. "I'll talk to Taylor," he said.

But how was still the question.

<hr>

Taylor had spent his whole day thinking about last night. It had made for a very distracting and occasionally uncomfortable workday. Trying to concentrate on Photoshop when hiding a hard-on under your desk was not productive, but that scene had been incredibly hot. He wanted to see Harold in nothing but a towel again. Who was he kidding? He wanted to see Harold in nothing, not even a towel. And his voice...that growl had been one of the sexiest things Taylor had ever heard. He was sure he could come on command if Harold used that voice. Hell, he had come on command last night.

It had been incredible. The challenge, the desperation, the threat of denial. So powerful and perfect. The only thing tarnishing the memory was the nervousness on Harold's face. It shouldn't have been there, and that was Taylor's fault. He'd pushed Harold into doing more than he was ready for. They'd never discussed pup play beyond simple things like cuddling on the couch, eating out of dog food bowls, and playing with toys. Harold was such a natural at being his Master that Taylor hadn't stopped to think about what he was doing before he did it. He needed to apologize.

He'd debated the whole subway ride home about how he'd do that but when he opened the door, the smell of fresh pizza wiped the words clean out of his brain.

"I'm starving," he said. He'd been so caught up with trying to work and daydreaming about Harold that he'd skipped lunch.

"You're right on time," Harold called from the living room. "It just came out of the oven."

"You made pizza?" Taylor asked as he shrugged off his coat and beelined for the coffee table.

"No," Harold said sheepishly. "But it is fresh."

"It looks delicious." Taylor grabbed a slice and bit into it with a moan. Melty cheese and warm bread. Was there anything better?

"You look ravenous."

"I skipped lunch," Taylor said, his mouth half-full.

"Try swallowing first."

Taylor grinned and devoured the rest of the slice. Harold picked up his own and bit into it more leisurely.

As Taylor's hunger abated, his brain came back online.

He set his third slice of pizza aside and opened his mouth to speak.

"Can we talk?" Harold asked.

Uh-oh. "About?" Taylor asked.

"Last night."

Shit. "I'm sorry. I shouldn't have pushed you."

"Pushed me?"

"To do something you weren't ready for."

"Oh."

Taylor cringed.

"Did you like it, though?" Harold asked.

"That's not the point."

"It is to me."

Taylor's train of thought halted in surprise. "What do you mean?"

"I mean I want you to like it. Whatever we're doing, I want you to get something out of it."

"What about you?"

Harold grinned. "It was fucking hot." He took a deep breath. "Not everything we do is like that. Whether you eat out of a dog bowl or a plate doesn't matter to me. But you like it. It's something you need, so..."

"You like giving it to me."

Harold nodded. It never ceased to amaze Taylor how much of a natural Dom he was.

"What was different about yesterday?" Taylor asked.

Harold's brow creased as he thought. Taylor took another bite of his pizza while he waited.

"Up until now, I've been on familiar ground. I don't know if you'll like what I'll do or if you'll want it until I try, but each idea has been something I would have done with Missy. Last night wasn't."

"You mean you never told Missy to hump a pillow until she came?" Taylor teased.

"Try the opposite."

That made sense. "How do we make it so you're not as nervous in the future?"

"That's a good question."

"We could map it all out. List our likes and dislikes, ideas, and boundaries, but I kind of like the organic flow we've had so far. It's...casual, relaxed."

"I like it too."

"Maybe it isn't scene specifics we need to figure out. Maybe it's sex."

"You said that pup play didn't always include sex," Harold said.

"Sometimes it does. Like last night."

"How do I know the difference?"

"For the most part, I think you can feel it out. My humping your bed was a good sign. When we're on the couch and you're petting my hair, that's not a sexual moment."

Harold nodded. "I can take my cues from you."

"Sometimes they might be blurry. In that case, you could always ask or suggest. Give me the option to choose if you can't tell."

"I can do that," Harold said. "Does this mean you want sexual scenes? With me, I mean."

Are you kidding? "Absolutely."

"What about sex?"

"As long as we're safe and both in the mood, you will find no objections from me. In fact, I have a request. Please pin me to the bed with those strong arms of yours."

Harold laughed. "Gladly."

Taylor waggled his eyebrows at him before picking up

the pizza again. They ate in silence for a while until they were both full.

"Anything else we should go over?" Taylor asked as they settled more comfortably on the couch.

"I spoke with James today. He mentioned discipline and punishments."

"Ah. Well, I'm not into structured rules," Taylor said. "A little scolding doesn't hurt. Like what you did last night or that time you were cooking."

"Cooking?"

"You scolded me for putting my paws up on the counter."

"Oh yeah," Harold said. "I used to do that to Missy all the time. She constantly begged for scraps."

"Seeing as you fed me, I'm assuming she didn't go away unsatisfied?"

"Nope. I'm a sucker."

"Noted," Taylor said with a smirk.

Harold rolled his eyes. "Last night I did more than scold you."

"Ah, yes. The pillow was a punishment. And you also almost sent me to bed with blue balls."

"Was that too much?"

"Hell no. I loved it. And I would have begged you in the morning to let me come if I had to."

"You wouldn't have touched yourself after you went to bed?"

"Nope. You'd told me I couldn't come unless it was that way. I'm a good pup. I listen to my Master."

"Somehow I think that's only sometimes true."

"Well..."

"You're okay with the punishment, though?"

"If I do something wrong or I'm being particularly

bratty, you're welcome to add a punishment to the scolding. But something fun. Not serious, please."

"Good," Harold said. "That's what I was hoping you'd say."

"That you're allowed to punish me?"

"That I wouldn't have to do so seriously. I'm not sure I could do that."

"Sounds like we're on the same page."

"Yeah." Harold was smiling; the nervousness Taylor had seen last night had vanished. "There's one more thing I'd like to ask before we finish this conversation."

"Shoot."

"When you go into...pup mode?"

Taylor nodded.

"You don't talk."

Taylor nodded again. "Human speech takes me out of the moment. As a pup, I prefer to bark or make gestures or sounds to communicate."

"I've noticed. And you're good at communicating like that, but we should invent some specific signals in case I need something clarified or if I'm not understanding something."

How had Harold never done BDSM or kink before? He was so freaking good at it. "That sounds like a great idea."

They spent the next hour discussing possible cues they could use and what each would mean. The conversation flowed comfortably, and it wasn't long before Taylor was lying with his head in Harold's lap as usual.

By the time they drifted to other topics, Taylor felt much better and no longer felt guilty. Harold seemed more confident about what they were doing, and Taylor eagerly anticipated seeing how that would factor into future scenes.

His excitement made work the following day drag on

endlessly. Now that they'd cleared the air, he wanted to put this new information into practice ASAP. Taylor was in the mood for something sexy. He hoped Harold was as well.

As he was leaving his desk for an overdue lunch break, Meisha, the photographer he worked with, waved to catch his attention.

"Pack your bags, Selby. We leave at 8:00 a.m. tomorrow."

"For what?"

"The May Morning project had a schedule change. We're headed to Florida for the next three days."

Three days? Taylor's hopes for a sexy scene crashed and burned. He didn't want to be away from Harold for three days. Not now. "Got it," he said. What else could he say?

When he finally arrived home, even the smell of chili couldn't lift his spirits.

"What's wrong with you?" Harold asked as he moped into the kitchen.

"My job is sending me to Florida for the next three days."

There was a momentary pause to Harold's stirring before he said, "Oh?"

"Yeah."

"Do you not like Florida?"

"It's not the destination," Taylor said.

"It's the time away?"

Taylor nodded. "I was hoping we could play now that we'd had that talk."

"So was I."

Taylor's mood brightened at that news. "Really?"

"What's the point of talking if we don't put words into action?"

Taylor sidled closer. "What did you have in mind?"

Harold glanced at him but quickly returned his focus to the pot. "Nothing you can't wait to find out after you get back."

"That's not fair."

"You have to wait either way."

"I want to know what I'm waiting for."

"Tell me tomorrow's winning lottery numbers, and I'll tell you what I'm planning."

"What kind of a request is that? I can't do that."

Harold shrugged. "Then I can't tell you."

"Yes, you can. I don't know the winning numbers, but you know what you're planning. There's a difference. In your case, it's possible."

"Oh no," Harold deadpanned. "I seem to have forgotten."

"I'd be happy to jostle the memory back into place for you." Taylor placed his hands on Harold's shoulders to intimate how that jostling would be achieved.

"That won't be necessary. You could get bowls and spoons out for us, and there's beer in the fridge."

Taylor reluctantly let go and went to set the table. On the way to the cabinet his phone beeped a text message alert.

Liam: Does this seem sketchy to you?

Following the message was an image of an ad reading:

Roommate/House Sitter Wanted

Looking for roommate/house sitter for a two-bedroom apartment in Tribeca. I am often away for work but will split a percentage of the rent and utilities. If interested, please call or text.

Taylor: Yes.
Liam: You're no help.
Taylor: Did you want me to say no?
Liam: I want you to come with me if I decide to check it out.
Taylor: First off, how are you going to afford this apartment?
Taylor: And second, I'm in Florida for the next three days.
Liam: What about when you get back?

I see we're ignoring reality, Taylor thought.

Taylor: Sure.

Liam was looking for a new place. It was more than Taylor had done, and Liam's text reminded him he was running out of time. He'd have to make a point to search for an apartment once he got back from Florida.

"Who was that?" Harold asked.

"My ex, Liam."

"What did he want?"

There was a touch of annoyance in Harold's tone, which Taylor thought unnecessary. It wasn't like Harold had met Liam or knew enough about him to be annoyed. Unless he was jealous? That was ridiculous. What would Harold have to be jealous about?

Taylor held up his phone to show Harold the image of the ad.

"That's sketchy."

"That's what I said."

"Is he going to answer it?"

"Not until I get home and can check it out with him."

"Why you?"

Before Taylor could retort *Why not me?* Harold said, "Never mind. Dinner's ready."

Confused, Taylor helped him bring the food to the coffee table. Although they ate and watched TV as always, Taylor's buoyant mood from the morning had well and truly deflated.

"What did you have in mind?"

"Nothing you can't wait to find out after you get back."

The answer to Taylor's question had been *nothing*. Harold had no idea what he wanted to do for a scene, and now that he'd implied he'd already planned something, he had three days to figure out what that something was.

"I'm fucked."

He considered calling James but didn't want to run to the man for help with every little detail of his relationship with Taylor. He was an adult. He could figure this out.

He couldn't figure this out.

His phone rang.

He half hoped it was James, but the screen said it was Madeline. "Hey, sis."

"Hey yourself."

"To what do I owe this pleasure?"

"Just checking in on my little brother. You are managing to get out of the house sometimes, right? Or is your new roommate keeping you too occupied to leave the bedroom? Please tell me you've taken advantage of hot and sexy."

"No, I have not taken advantage of hot and sexy." *Though I made him hump a pillow.*

"Well, that's disappointing. What are you waiting for?"

"He's away for business for the next three days."

"That sucks," she said. "Wait, that doesn't explain why you haven't been banging his brains out before now. What's wrong with him?"

"Nothing's wrong with him," Harold protested.

"Something's obviously wrong if he's still sleeping on your couch. Is it you? Did Sean kill your libido with boredom, and now you don't know how to get it going again when things are exciting?"

"My libido is fine, thank you."

"Then why aren't you getting any?"

"Why don't you go get some and stay out of my business?"

"Do you honestly think I'm capable of mad monkey sex? I have a full-time job, a child, and thin walls in my home. When the fuck do I have time for that? I need to live vicariously through you. Now get on it!"

"I'm working on it," Harold admitted. "I have to wait until he's back, though."

"I expect a full report next week."

"Hell no."

"Can you at least let me know if it went well so I can be happy for you?" she asked.

"That I can do."

"Good. Now tell me what's bothering you."

"What?"

"We got the fun stuff out of the way. Now you can tell me what's worrying you."

"Nothing's worrying me."

"Liar. I can tell when something's on your mind."

He wasn't going to tell her he was trying to figure out a kinky scene for Taylor in the hopes it would lead to sex, but reminding himself of his current dilemma brought up another concern he could share. "What if I go for the hot monkey sex and end up wanting more?" he asked. "What if I end up wanting it to be permanent?"

"Oh, Harold…"

The sympathy in her voice was too much. "I didn't say I was, so you can stop with the pity party. It's just a question."

Neither of them believed that. Harold had never been one to do casual relationships in the past. It was unlikely he'd start now.

"When's your deadline?" she asked.

"Three weeks."

"You should make the most of these weeks and see what happens. If he's recently out of a relationship, he might not be ready for another one yet. Especially one that starts with you living together. I'd say enjoy the time you have but try not to get your hopes too high."

That was reasonable. How many relationships began with the couple moving in together days after they met? "Thanks, sis."

"Anytime. Oh, and I'm still waiting for a picture of this young hottie of yours."

"Still not giving one to you."

"Come on. How can I live vicariously if I don't know what I'm working with?"

"Use your imagination."

"Do I at least get a name for this person? Or should I call him hot and sexy forever?"

Harold laughed. "His name is Taylor."

"Taylor. Got it." There was a ruckus in the background on her end. "Shit. Got to go. I'll talk to you later, baby brother. Love you."

"Love you, too."

Harold could make the most of the time he had with

Taylor. Limited as it was, he believed it would be worth it. Taylor had already brought more joy into his life than he'd had for years. He'd deal with the aftermath when it came.

If he was going to put his all into their time, he needed to start planning. Suddenly, he knew exactly where to start. He grabbed his laptop and entered *BDSM pup play kneepads* into his browser search. He got lost in the rabbit hole of the internet, finding all sorts of information about various pieces of pup gear. It was fascinating, the varying degrees people's outfits took when they did this. Some were covered from head to toe, giving a full illusion of an animal. Others were in the bare minimum. He wondered what Taylor liked and what he might have worn besides his pup mask.

One of his detours from his original search was into the land of tails. Taylor would look good with a tail, and he decided to poke around to see what was available. At first he thought he'd like one with fur, but they mostly hung like a ponytail down the models' asses. When he pictured Taylor in a tail, he imagined something that curved up, like a dog's when it was happy. He couldn't find anything like that with fur, though, only skinny silicone things that mostly came in black. He didn't like them, but when he found one that wagged and was controlled by a wireless remote, he changed his mind. He could definitely picture Taylor wearing that with his mask.

And nothing else.

He checked the site he was currently on for shipping details. If he could get it in time for Taylor's return...

It was sold out.

Harold felt like the world was reminding him not to get his hopes up too high. He returned to his original search for kneepads and found a slip-on pair where the pads were shaped like dog paws. He added them to his cart, checked out, and pushed the computer away.

In need of a break, he got up to make coffee, promising himself that when he sat back down again, he'd focus on work. Ten minutes later, mug in hand, Harold opened his laptop again, ready to tackle Python instead of kink. As soon as he'd begun to successfully concentrate, his phone rang.

Mixed signals much, universe?

He glanced at the screen. James was calling.

"Hello?"

"Hello, Harold. I hope I'm not interrupting."

"It's all right."

"I wanted to discuss that project I mentioned and see if you were still interested in taking it."

"Cyber security, right?"

"Yes."

It was far from Harold's favorite thing to do, but work was work. "Sure. Would this be for your home? An office? Something else?"

"My home. I would like to have my network secure so I may freelance from here."

"What are you planning on doing?"

"I'm still working out the details, but I thought I'd be prepared."

"Were you a Boy Scout?"

James laughed. "No. If I had been, perhaps my plans wouldn't have gone awry as often as they did."

"Can't account for everything," Harold said.

"We try our best, though, don't we?"

"Professionally? Yes."

"And how are things going personally?"

"Taylor's away for a few days, but we did get to talk before he left."

"How'd that go?"

"It went well. I'm feeling much steadier," Harold said. "I did sort of promise him a scene when he gets home, and I have no idea what to do for it."

"With what I know of Taylor, you don't have to plan anything big or elaborate. His pleasure is derived from the playing."

"But what we've done so far hasn't been much. I'm sure he wants more."

"More doesn't mean different," James said.

"What do you mean?"

"You said you've been stepping cautiously until now, correct?" James asked.

"Yes."

"What would you have done in those scenes if you hadn't been holding back?"

Harold thought for a moment, and his fantasy came back to him, the one where he'd imagined Taylor sucking him off after sleeping on his lap. It was a hot fantasy, one he'd love to make real, but some of the details were a big jump to take from where he stood.

"I might still want to step cautiously," Harold said.

"You can, but you can walk a little farther, can't you?"

"Yeah." He'd done that when making Taylor masturbate with a pillow.

"Push where you feel comfortable doing so. Don't worry about the rest," James said. "And know you are welcome to call me anytime if you have questions."

"Thank you."

"You're welcome. Would you be able to stop by tomorrow to look over my network and computer?"

It took a second for Harold to switch gears back into

work mode. "Sure. Text me your address, and I'll stop by in the morning."

"I have a few errands to run. Let's say around ten?"

"You got it."

Harold tried to focus on work after hanging up with James, but it was no use. His brain refused to concentrate. After struggling for an hour, he gave up and grabbed his gym bag. Sometimes exercise helped when his mind was feeling particularly scatterbrained. Today it was unable to think of anything but Taylor.

***

Taylor loved his job. He loved what he did, and he liked the people he did it with, but three days away from Harold fixed a dark cloud over his enthusiasm. He tried his best not to show it, pumping his professionalism to the max, but whenever he had a moment to stop and think, it was there waiting for him, a personal storm filled with doubt and anxiety.

What if Harold didn't want to do pup play after all? What if he preferred to stick with their cuddle time on the couch? What if he decided he didn't want to do anything with Taylor at all? The thoughts spiraled from there into what if he changed his mind about Taylor staying with him and Taylor had to go back to his apartment?

The questions were illogical, but he couldn't stop them. He'd just managed to open the door to doing more with Harold. What if that door shut before he had a chance to step through it?

He longed to call Harold. These relentless thoughts would wash away with the sound of his voice, but it'd only been six hours since he'd landed.

I can't call him so soon after seeing him. How desperate would that look?

Instead, he wallowed, he worried, and he tried to distract himself with photographing a very attractive male model. When said model wasn't being directed to look elsewhere, his eyes often turned Taylor's way. Taylor thought he saw interest in the man's gaze, but although he was very good-looking, he wasn't Harold.

I miss him. How can I miss him when I've only been gone half a day? My workdays at home are longer than this.

But those workdays ended with Harold's home-cooked meals and his company. Today would end with a restaurant picked by majority rule and cold hotel sheets.

As they paused for a fifteen-minute break, Taylor put his equipment down and took out his phone. His finger automatically landed on the sensor from years of habit, and it unlocked. His thumb hovered over the text message app, but he didn't open it.

What would I say anyway?

"You look like a lost puppy."

Taylor startled and looked up. The model, Roland, was standing next to him holding a bottle of water. He held it out to Taylor. "Want something to drink?"

"I'm fine, thanks," Taylor said.

"Sorry about the crazy schedule. I hope it didn't ruin any plans."

Yes, I was looking forward to finding out what Harold as a pup Master was like. And sex. I was really looking forward to some sex.

Taylor shrugged. "Changes happen."

"So there's no disappointed significant other back home cursing me out for taking you away?"

How to answer that? Taylor didn't want to lead him on, but he was too nice to flat-out lie. "It's complicated."

Roland laughed. "Isn't it always? Does your complicated allow you to have dinner with me tonight?"

"I probably shouldn't."

Roland nodded. "Didn't hurt to ask."

"Thank you," Taylor said. "For asking."

Roland headed back toward the refreshment table where his manager rushed over to speak with him. Taylor watched him go, then turned back to his phone. His feelings while looking at it were even more complicated now. What was he to Harold? And vice versa? Were they free to see other people? Were they technically together or was this just a roommate and kink thing? He should take a page from Joanne's method for relationships. Despite the variety, each of her relationships was clearly defined and committed for the length of their duration. There was an efficiency to them Taylor would never be able to manage, but he had to admit that orderliness kept most of the drama Joanne would otherwise encounter out of her life. He might not be as businesslike about it as her, but he should have added a few items to the conversation he'd had with Harold before he left. If things were getting more involved between them, they'd have to discuss those details as well.

"Break's over!" someone called. It was time to get back to work.

After the obligatory group dinner, Taylor returned to the room he was sharing with another assistant and flopped onto the bed. He pulled his phone out of his pocket and rolled onto his back. He wanted to text Harold, but he didn't know what to say. Finally, he settled on something he considered innocuous enough.

Taylor: Had taquitos tonight. Weren't as good as yours.

He waited five minutes but didn't receive a reply. Disappointed, he headed into the bathroom for a shower. He still hadn't received a response when he got out. Frustrated, he threw the phone on the bed and grabbed his laptop to pull up Netflix. Nothing appealed to him.

"This is what boyfriends are good for," he muttered.

Usually, he'd call Liam when he was on a location shoot and bored. Even if Liam was in the middle of a video game, he'd chat distractedly with Taylor, or Taylor would listen to the noises of the game in the background. He didn't need an in-depth conversation. It was the company he missed.

Harold wasn't his boyfriend. They weren't even friends. Or were they? What were they?

"Fuck it." He grabbed his phone again and dialed. Harold picked up after the third ring.

"Hello?"

"Hi."

There was an awkward silence.

"Am I interrupting anything?" Taylor asked.

"Nope. Just got out of the shower."

"Same here."

Another silence.

"How was the shoot?" Harold asked.

"It was okay. The model tried to pick me up."

"Oh?"

Was there something in Harold's voice or was Taylor imagining it? "Yeah, I turned him down, though."

"Not hot enough?"

"Not the right kind of hot."

"What's the right kind of hot?"

You are. "Someone"—Taylor's lips curled into a smirk—"who'd make me hump a pillow until I came."

"James then."

"What? No! Well, yes, but that's not what I was thinking."

"Thinking of someone in particular, were you?"

"Maybe." Taylor felt much better now. They were flirting. Harold still liked him. Harold wasn't going to send him away, and Taylor didn't feel lonely. "I—" *I miss you.* "I'm still looking forward to that scene when I get back."

"Don't get your hopes up too high. It's not going to be anything elaborate."

"Doesn't have to be," Taylor said. "I know whatever you do, I'll like it."

Harold let out a breath. "I'm glad to hear you say that."

"Were you worried?" Taylor asked, surprised.

"Yes."

"Why?"

"Because this is new, and up until now you were the one leading. I haven't had to come up with ideas on my own."

"Do you want to talk about it?" Taylor asked. "Plan something together?"

"No, I think I've figured it out. Just...bear with me. I'll probably be a little nervous."

"You were nervous last time, and you still managed to blow my mind," Taylor pointed out.

Harold let out a soft laugh. "Good to know."

"Now I'm really curious. I can't wait to get home."

"You'll have to suffer with the anticipation."

Taylor pouted. "You can't give me a little taste over the phone?"

"I am not having phone sex with you."

"Does this mean the scene includes sex?" Taylor asked excitedly.

"No, but I can't get you to play with a ball or pet you over the phone. What else is there to do?"

"You make it sound like a consolation prize. What sort of sex have you been having?"

"Not good sex, according to my sister."

"Do I want to know how your sister knows that?"

"Stop making weird assumptions."

"You brought it up," Taylor said.

"And now I'm un-bringing it up," Harold retorted.

"Un-bringing is not a word."

"It is today."

"Are you sure you won't have phone sex with me?" Taylor asked.

"Yes, I'm sure."

"Bet all this talk has made you hard, though," Taylor teased.

"Not enough to change my mind."

"But a little?"

Harold sighed.

"Oh, come on. Tell me," Taylor begged.

There was a pause and then Harold spoke, his voice seductively low. "I am in my bedroom, sitting on my bed in nothing but a towel. There's a bottle of lube and a dildo in my nightstand drawer that I plan to reacquaint myself with for the next few hours." Taylor gasped. "I will do so loudly and enthusiastically." Taylor moaned. "But I will not do it on the phone with you. Good night, Taylor."

"Wait, what?" By the time Taylor had caught up, the

dial tone was already ringing in his ear. He disconnected the call and quickly texted *ASSHOLE!* Harold's reply was a series of laughing emojis.

Taylor tossed his phone aside and face planted into his pillow. His mind was flooded with images of Harold masturbating. Had he used the dildo the night Taylor had overheard him? Taylor groaned. He wanted to watch Harold jerk off. He hoped that was part of the plan for when he returned.

Chapter Ten

The following two days were still difficult but made better by nightly phone calls with Harold. They never spoke about anything important, but that wasn't the point. The conversations were a connection, and they kept Taylor's anxiety at bay. They also made him impatient to see Harold in person again. By the time he was on a plane home, he was restless with anticipation.

"Your knee is bouncing again," Meisha said.

"Sorry." Taylor couldn't help it. He'd see Harold in a matter of hours, and they were going to scene. He had no idea what that was going to entail or when exactly it would happen, but Harold had hinted it would happen tonight.

The wait for his luggage was interminably long, though it was probably only ten minutes. The taxi ride also took forever, but he finally arrived at Harold's apartment. He unlocked the door and shoved it open.

"I'm ba—" His announcement cut short when he saw Harold standing in the foyer.

"Welcome home," Harold said.

Home. "Thank you." The warmth from the word

contrasted with confusion. Why was Harold standing in the doorway? Should he enter?

"How was your flight?" Harold asked.

"It was okay. No issues at least." He'd barely noticed the flight, too focused on getting home. *Home*, Taylor thought the word again. It felt so good to hear. It felt right.

"Are you jet-lagged or anything?"

"Not really. A little hungry maybe." Why were they talking while Taylor was still in the hall?

Harold nodded. "Do you want to eat now, or can you wait a while?"

"I can wait." Taylor suspected there was more to Harold's questions than their simplicity suggested.

"How—" Harold began but cut off the question. "Good. Come in." He stepped aside so Taylor could enter. "I'm going to start a bath. I'd like you to join me in the bathroom after you drop off your luggage and jacket."

Join him? Taylor's confusion cleared as he realized Harold was starting the scene. He was awkward in his setup, but Taylor could tell he was trying his best. The questions must have been Harold feeling him out to see if Taylor would be up for whatever he had in mind. Taylor smiled. "I'd be happy to."

That seemed to relax Harold. He smiled in return, and with another nod, he headed into the bathroom.

Taylor dropped his stuff in the corner of the living room but didn't immediately follow. He wasn't in pup mode, and he didn't know how easily he'd be able to drop into it. Despite his anticipation for the scene, his mind was still wrapped up in work and the plane ride. He needed to let that go before he could be a pup. Harold seemed to under-stand that. He had to trust that whatever Harold had in mind would help him get there. He took a deep breath and followed Harold into the bathroom.

Inside the bathroom, Harold had started the bath. He crouched by the side of the tub, one hand under the running water, testing the temperature. When it was sufficiently hot but not scalding, he plugged the drain and let it fill. Taylor entered while he was waiting.

"Everything all right?" he asked. He needed to know Taylor was up for doing this so quickly after he came home. It was his primary concern. He was surprised to find it was his only concern. Beyond that, he wasn't nervous about the scene at all. He hadn't been since that first night he'd spoken to Taylor over the phone.

Earlier that day he'd fretted constantly. Even wearing himself out at the gym hadn't helped, but as soon as he'd heard Taylor's voice, all the worry had washed away. There hadn't been anything earth-shattering to change how he'd felt, but the natural ease with which they'd flirted and teased made him realize it wasn't what they did that mattered. At the heart of every scene they'd had so far was Harold giving Taylor what he needed. As long as he did that, he'd be fine, and at this point Harold was reasonably confident he could do that. He'd had plenty of practice learning to read him and knew what he liked.

"Yes, Sir," Taylor said.

Sir. Harold took that as Taylor's way of telling him he was on board with the scene. "I'd like you to take off your clothes and set them aside," he said, keeping his eyes on the water. It was going to be difficult enough seeing Taylor naked and wet in the tub, but his focus wasn't on sex right now. He wanted to let Taylor unwind after his time away.

He heard the rustling of fabric as Taylor followed directions.

When the water was finally high enough, he turned off the faucet and shifted aside. "You can step in." Taylor came forward and dipped a toe in the water before sliding one leg in and then the other. "Sit down and get comfortable," Harold said. Taylor lowered himself down, a sigh of pleasure escaping him as he leaned back against the side of the tub. His eyes closed, and Harold let him savor the sensation.

With the way the bathroom was set up, Harold could sit on the closed toilet lid and be next to Taylor's head. He settled onto the makeshift seat and ran his fingers through Taylor's hair. Taylor sighed.

"That's it. Relax. You've had a long week. All you have to do tonight is enjoy."

A smile curved Taylor's lips. Harold continued petting him.

"I had a long week as well," Harold said. "I started a project for James. I don't think I told you. He wants me to look over the security at his apartment, network stuff mostly. I thought it would be boring, but the technology that man owns is unexpected. Makes me wonder what he used to do at his previous job."

Taylor's eyelids fluttered open to look at him.

"You don't have to speak. I'm only rambling."

Taylor's lips parted as if he were going to speak.

"I know you're not in pup mode," Harold said.

Taylor smiled again and closed his eyes.

"Good boy." Harold resumed his petting.

After a while, he lifted Taylor's arm, turning his hand

over to see if his fingers had turned pruney. They were just beginning to wrinkle.

"Can you sit up for me?" he asked.

Taylor was drowsy but managed to listen to directions. Harold reached for the bottle of shampoo he'd set aside and poured some into his palm. He spread it between his hands, then began working it into Taylor's hair. Taylor let out a groan.

"Like that?" Harold teased. He massaged Taylor's scalp as he worked, eliciting more sounds of delight from the younger man. When his head was fully lathered, Harold used a small bucket to scoop up water from the tub and pour it over Taylor's head. Once clean, he performed the same action with conditioner. Taylor left himself completely to Harold's ministrations. If it weren't for the noises he made, Harold would have thought he was asleep.

Finished, he said, "Time to rinse off."

This time the noise Taylor made wasn't of happiness.

"Don't worry, we're not done yet."

He assisted Taylor to stand and unplugged the drain. Rinsing him quickly, he wrapped Taylor in a towel and had him sit on the toilet. Taking another towel, he massaged Taylor's head as he dried his hair. The blissful sounds returned, this time with words. "Feels so good."

"I'm glad you like it," Harold said.

When Taylor's hair was no longer drippy, Harold ushered him into the living room where a nest of blankets awaited him on the couch. Taylor burrowed straight into the pile.

"I'm going to make us dinner. You'll be all right waiting here?"

The mound of blankets nodded.

Harold smiled. Even when we wasn't being a pup, Taylor could still be as adorable as one.

He went into the kitchen and began cooking. The familiar actions let him take a mental step back to assess the scene so far.

Harold wasn't always in the best of moods after traveling. In case Taylor was the same way, he'd focused on letting Taylor relax and unwind. He figured something like this could work whether it was pup play or not. So far, it seemed he was right.

Next, he'd feed Taylor, then, depending on Taylor's mood, they'd either play or relax some more. He'd planned a general structure for the scene but left the details open so he could be flexible. Even when he was the one arranging things, he still followed Taylor's lead.

As he turned off the burner, he considered what bowls to take out of the cabinet. He'd made skillet veal, which could easily be eaten from Taylor's dog bowl, if a little messily. He'd wanted Taylor to have the option. The question was how to ask him what he wanted. If Taylor didn't want to speak, Harold didn't want to force him to.

In the end he poured Taylor's portion into his dog bowl and brought a spoon in case he wanted to use it. Out in the living room, the pile of blankets hadn't moved.

"Have you fallen asleep under there?"

The blankets shook drowsily in the negative.

"Time for dinner."

After some movement and shifting, Taylor's head poked out from the blankets. He looked blearily at Harold.

"You have the option to eat from your bowl on the floor or where you are with a spoon. What do you want to do?"

Taylor took a minute before answering, then crawled down to the floor, taking some of the blankets with him.

Harold set the bowl in front of him and patted him on the head before moving to the couch to eat his own food.

He watched Taylor as they ate, drinking in the sight of him. It soothed the part of him that had missed the young man's company.

Taylor was impressed with Harold's choices in the scene so far. It was clear he hadn't been expecting Taylor to be in pup mode and accounted for it. The bath and Harold's pampering had lulled him into a snuggly comfort and washed away the harried stresses of travel. While under the blankets, Taylor had begun to feel a little playful but mostly sleepy. Now that he'd had food, he was energized and awake. He wanted to *do* something. He wanted to move around, stretch, have fun. Perhaps it was partially due to eating from his bowl, but Taylor was in the mood for pup time. And so, when he finished eating, he turned to Harold and barked. He bounded out of the blankets and over to Harold on the couch. He hadn't been able to avoid smearing his mouth with sauce from dinner. Now it worked in his favor as he licked a wet, messy kiss over Harold's cheek.

"Down, pup! Down!" Harold ordered, laughing. "We need to clean you up before you can play."

Taylor wasn't in the mood to listen. He followed Harold's direction back onto the floor, then turned around and rested his front paws on Harold's knees and barked again.

"I said down, pup," Harold said. "Or you won't get your present."

Present? Taylor lowered his paws to the floor. *What present?*

"That's what I thought. Now wait here like a good boy."

Taylor waited.

When Harold returned, his first action was to attack Taylor's face with a damp paper towel. Taylor squirmed to avoid it, his nose scrunched up unhappily. *That's not a present!*

"Patience, pup. Let me clean your face. Then you will get your present. You might want to wear your mask with it, and we can't have you getting sauce on your mask, can we?"

Taylor calmed down and let Harold clean his face, but he still scrunched his nose to show his displeasure.

Harold laughed. "Your complaint is noted," he said.

Finally clean, Taylor looked at Harold expectantly.

"Okay, pup." Harold set the paper towel aside and pulled out a box, the kind packages were mailed in. Had he ordered something while Taylor was away? Or had he gotten it before Taylor left?

Harold reached into the box and pulled out something black in clear plastic. He ripped open the plastic and held out the objects—there were two of them—so Taylor could see.

"I hope they fit and feel comfortable," Harold said.

Taylor's eyes widened. They were kneepads! And they had paw-shaped cushions! Taylor barked happily. He wanted to wear them and play.

"Come on up here and lie back so we can try them on."

Taylor eagerly did as told, and soon his knees were wrapped in soft cotton and his kneecaps were shielded by plush paws. He rolled off the couch to try crawling on them. He had to return to Harold for a slight adjustment on his right knee, but then they were perfect.

"I think it's ball time, don't you?"

Taylor barked his agreement.

"Do you want your mask?"

Yes, he did. He went over to his belongings and nosed the bag he kept it in. It was closed, so he whined for Harold to get the mask for him. Harold obliged and before long he was geared up and playing ball. Harold sat back on the couch to watch, occasionally tossing the ball when requested, but mostly Taylor entertained himself.

"All you're missing is a tail."

Taylor agreed. He'd love to have a tail one day, but he'd worry about that later. It wasn't a necessity. Right now, nosing his ball into place so he could bite it was.

"I suppose the one without fur wouldn't be so bad."

Taylor froze. *The one without fur?*

"It'd look hot, actually."

Taylor was still hung up on the words "the one" to pay much attention to the compliment. If there was one without fur, did that mean there was one with? And did that mean Harold had been looking at tails as well as kneepads?

Taylor's heart felt full. He'd never had anyone want to buy him a tail before. He'd never had anyone buy him any pup gear before. He'd saved for his mask and any kneepads he'd used were borrowed.

Harold wanted to buy him gear, as if Taylor were really his pup. Taylor abandoned the ball and hurried to the couch. He prodded his Master's knee, wanting to express his appreciation and the feelings that were trying to burst from inside him.

Thank you. Thank you, thank you, thank you.

It wasn't enough, but Taylor didn't know what else to do.

He felt Harold's hand on the back of his head and nudged again while being petted.

"I take it you like the idea of a tail?" Harold asked.

Taylor felt this moment was too precious to ruin by barking. He nuzzled closer.

"I do like the idea of seeing you in one," Harold said.

He did? Taylor shifted to see if Harold's enjoyment was more than aesthetic. The tenting of his jeans made it clear it was. He moved to the other side of Harold's knee, gently urging Harold to part his legs. Harold did, and Taylor rubbed his cheek on the inside of Harold's thigh.

"Taylor? What are you doing?"

Taylor decided the question was rhetorical as the answer was fairly obvious. He pushed forward. Warmth brushed a ghost of a kiss against his lips, and he licked them. He wanted to press in farther, smell his Master, taste him, but he couldn't do that without permission.

"This wasn't meant to be sex time, pup. I don't want you to do anything you don't want to. You don't have to worry about me."

But Taylor wanted to. He whined and nuzzled again. *Please let me, Master. I want to. I really want to.*

The muscles beneath his cheek clenched and released. A moment later, Harold's legs widened.

"Go ahead, pup."

It was like his fantasy, only more intense because it was real. It took every ounce of willpower Harold had not to shove Taylor's face into his groin.

He didn't have to. Now given permission, his pup leaned in the rest of the way, pressing the nose of the mask against Harold's erection. He heard Taylor inhale deeply, and that was fucking hot.

Taylor rubbed his nose back and forth over Harold's

erection, then nudged forward as if he wanted to get even closer. He whined again.

"Having a little trouble there, pup?" Harold couldn't help teasing.

Another whine.

"How about you try a little harder?"

There was nothing stopping Taylor from using his hands and taking what he wanted, but as a pup, Harold knew he wouldn't. Like the time with the pillow, Taylor's struggle stimulated Harold, both mentally and physically. He enjoyed it for a while before asking, "Would you like some help?"

Taylor made a noise of agreement.

"You have to let me know what you want then or I won't be able to help you."

Taylor nuzzled again.

"You can't get any closer than that, pup." Harold petted the back of Taylor's head. "Let's see... You've been doing well smelling me. You seemed to like that. I know you can touch me; I feel you just fine with all that wriggling. It can't be sound since you can hear me when I ask you questions. Perhaps it's taste. Do you want to taste me, pup?" Taylor wiggled more urgently, making desperate, needy noises. "All right, pup," Harold said, his voice hoarse with his own anticipation. "Give me some room and I'll help."

Taylor reluctantly sat back, allowing Harold the space he needed to reach down and unzip his pants. He pushed his underwear out of the way—why hadn't he learned from his fantasy and skipped wearing any—and pulled out his erection. Taylor's eyes were transfixed on it, and his hungry gaze left Harold breathless.

"It's all yours," he whispered.

Taylor dove for it. There was no better word to describe

how fast he moved. He swallowed Harold's dick in one smooth motion, plunging forward as far as he could go.

"Oh fuck!" Harold exclaimed. It'd been a long time since he'd had a warm mouth around his cock, and Taylor's was amazing. He sucked and licked as if he couldn't get enough. Harold fought hard not to thrust deeper.

Noticing his resistance, Taylor paused and rolled his eyes up to look at Harold. He made a questioning sound.

"It's okay, pup. You do as you like."

Taylor pleaded.

"You want me to? I don't think I could go slow, baby. I'm itching for hard and fast."

Taylor whined again.

"All right," Harold said. "Put your paws on my thighs. If it becomes too much, squeeze them to let me know."

Taylor did as told, the action so trusting it rocked Harold to his core.

"Here we go, baby."

Holding Taylor's head in place, he did as he'd warned. He thrust hard and fast into Taylor's mouth. It was beyond anything he'd ever done before, rough and ruthless, and Taylor took it with moans of encouragement. It was exhilarating to let go like that, and soon he'd shoved forward to come down Taylor's throat.

"Holy fuck." He gasped as he slumped back onto the couch. He would have rested there for a good stretch of time if Taylor hadn't begun rubbing his face urgently against his leg. Concerned something was wrong, Harold helped him get the mask off.

"What's wro—"

Before he could finish the question, Taylor had climbed into his lap, grabbed his face, and kissed him. The kiss was hard, hot, and open-mouthed, as if his pup was set to devour him. He could taste his semen on Taylor's tongue, and he chased it until the flavor disappeared.

Among the ravishing kisses, he could feel Taylor's erection pressed against him. His pup was desperately hard, smearing pre-cum with each movement. Harold took hold of his cock, and Taylor thrust into his grip.

"That's it," Harold coaxed. "Come for me."

It didn't take long before Taylor did. His body jerked as he came, and he collapsed, spent, against Harold's shoulder. He didn't stay for long, as Harold had expected, but wriggled back off the couch and onto the floor. Before Harold could question why, Taylor licked his cum clean from where it had fallen on Harold's clothes. Fascinated, Harold held out his hand, and he licked that too.

"Damn, that's hot," Harold breathed.

When Taylor was finished, Harold turned to lie back on the couch. "Up, pup. I want to hold you."

Taylor came up and lay half on top of him. Harold wrapped him in his arms, feeling his warmth and smooth skin. His towel was long gone, and he wasn't wearing anything but kneepads. Not wanting Taylor to get cold, Harold reached for one of the many blankets around them and covered them both with it.

"We're going to stay like this for a while, okay?"

Taylor nodded, snuggling closer, and Harold smiled. This felt so right, so perfect. And after the most intense sex he'd ever had in his life too!

Man, he was fucked. That three-week deadline could go to hell.

Taylor must have dozed off because he jolted awake to find Harold looking at him.

"It's time for bed, pup," Harold said.

Taylor frowned. He didn't want to leave this warm space and Harold's company. The bedroom was so far away. After such a wonderful scene, it felt like the Grand Canyon of distances. How could he abide that sort of separation?

"Would you be okay sleeping at the foot of my bed?" Harold asked.

What? It took a moment for Taylor to process Harold's question. When he did, a thrill went through him. Harold really had thought of everything with this scene. No, it wasn't the scene. He'd thought of Taylor. Everything he'd done was focused on Taylor, his needs, his mood, his desires. It made Taylor feel amazing and cared for.

He nodded. *Yes, let's not separate.*

They had to if only to get off the couch and into Harold's bedroom. Taylor brought his favorite blanket and a pillow with him. He dropped it on the bed and immediately crawled on and made himself comfortable. Harold laughed and pulled back the covers.

"At least you left me some space," he said as he lay down.

Once he was settled, Taylor wriggled closer until he was lying against Harold's legs. He was happy to be in the bedroom, but it wasn't enough. He needed touch.

He felt Harold's fingers in his hair. "All right, pup?"

Yes. Taylor nodded. *Much better now.*

He was smiling as he drifted off to sleep.

Chapter Eleven

Harold woke up hard and aching. Given the events of the previous evening, it was no wonder. He reached for his cock and gave it a tug. The stimulation made him bite his lip with a groan. He lazily stroked himself through his pants as he replayed various moments from last night in his mind. He wanted to do them again. Hell, he wanted to do all of it again, even the parts that hadn't been sexual. It'd been really nice taking care of Taylor. He wanted to care for him more.

You won't be able to do that forever, a voice inside his head reminded him. *Don't go getting your hopes up. Enjoy the opportunities you have now before they're gone.*

He pushed the thoughts aside and returned his attention to the indolent pleasure he was giving himself.

A whimper reminded him he wasn't the only one in the bed. He hadn't forgotten, but the knowledge that Taylor was probably watching him made him suddenly shy, and he stopped moving. He opened his eyes and looked toward the foot of the bed. Taylor was curled up in a ball beneath his blanket, his gaze fixed on the lump that was clearly Harold's hand on his cock under the covers.

"I—"

Taylor made another soft noise, and there was a plea in his eyes. Harold wasn't sure what he was asking for. He thought it safe to assume Taylor was in pup mode since he wasn't talking. What would Taylor as a pup want from him right now?

Treat me like you would Missy.

If Missy had been there, Harold wouldn't have felt embarrassed about masturbating. He would have kicked her off the bed and set to enjoying himself. He wasn't going to send Taylor away, but perhaps Taylor was saying he could continue. Maybe he wanted to watch.

Harold had never masturbated in front of anyone. No matter how well Taylor became a dog when he was in pup mode, he was still a person in reality and counted as such.

I can do this. It'll probably be hot.

He gave his cock an experimental stroke. Taylor didn't make another sound, but his eyes were transfixed by the movement.

Keep going, Harold told himself.

He did. It was weird having an audience, especially one so rapt. Harold became more focused on Taylor than on his own dick. With his actions out of sight, he felt emboldened to slip his hand under the waistband of his pj's. He groaned at the luscious touch of skin, his attention shifting to pleasure once more and his embarrassment fading even further. He stroked faster, not caring that Taylor knew exactly what he was doing.

Taylor made a whine and pawed at the bedspread. Harold acknowledged the movement, but his brain was too fogged to translate. Taylor did it again, drawing his paw toward himself a few times. His fingers were curled, and they caught on the fabric as they slid over it.

I think he wants to see more.

With his free hand, Harold lifted the blankets out of the way so Taylor had an unobstructed view as he continued stroking. He was beyond embarrassment now, his need overriding any sense of caution or self-consciousness. Taylor licked his lips as he watched, and Harold was reminded of the warmth of his mouth, the tight suction, and his teasing tongue.

Will he take me in his mouth again if I let him?

Taylor shifted and crawled closer. He kept his eyes on Harold, waiting to see if each step was approved before taking another. Harold let him approach until he was close enough to nip the waistband of Harold's pajamas.

He wants to see more. He might want to do more than see.

The thought made him ache. He gave a sharp nod, and Taylor leaned forward again, taking the edge of Harold's pants between his teeth and tugging. He pulled down as far as he could go, which wasn't much. Harold lifted his hips, allowing Taylor to pull farther. Taylor did, wiggling backward when his head couldn't move low enough. The fact that he didn't use his hands at all turned Harold on something fierce, and when Harold's erection was finally exposed, it was dripping with pre-cum and throbbing.

"Are you as hard as I am, pup?"

Taylor grunted and rocked his hips as if trying to gain friction on the bed.

"Let me feel you. Come closer."

Taylor crawled forward and Harold reached a hand beneath him to cup his cock and balls. His dick was hot and dabbled with pre-cum.

"Watching me turned you on, huh?" The knowledge made Harold feel good.

Taylor nuzzled his shoulder.

He toyed with Taylor's erection for a bit, enjoying how it made his pup squirm. "Do you want to do more than watch, pup? Do you want to taste?"

Taylor made a pleading noise.

"Let's make this a little easier then, shall we?" Harold maneuvered his pants off and tossed them to the floor. He shoved the blankets farther out of the way and said, "Go ahead, baby. Crawl between my legs and play."

Taylor licked a kiss on Harold's cheek before wriggling backward down the bed and moving between Harold's legs. He lapped gently at the head of Harold's cock. It was sexy as fuck and torturous as hell. "Do it again," Harold ordered.

Taylor did. With small licks, he tasted Harold's erection like it was a bowl of water. He cleaned the pre-cum that had dripped down the shaft, then moved to Harold's balls and cleaned them too. It wasn't enough to get Harold off, but it was so good.

"More, pup. I want more."

He wanted tight heat and strong friction. He wanted to come, but Taylor kept his ministrations simple, and they were going to drive him insane. When Taylor's tongue licked a stripe in the crease where Harold's thigh met his groin, he couldn't take it anymore. He left his balls to Taylor and took hold of his cock, jerking it fast, yet it still wasn't enough. When Taylor nuzzled his balls, lifting them with his nose, Harold knew what he wanted.

Yes.

He lifted his legs, granting his pup permission. The first touch of that tongue to his hole sent fire through his body and he cried out, "Oh fuck! Yes!" His hand moved frantically. He was so close; he just needed a little more to get over the edge. "Stick it in, pup. Stick it in, now." Taylor pushed his tongue into his hole. It didn't go far, but it was enough. Harold's orgasm ripped through him like a tornado, and he cried out. Drops of cum splattered his chest. One even hit him on his chin. He kept going until he was fully empty and then dropped his legs to the mattress.

He kept his eyes closed during his post-orgasm bliss, aware of Taylor licking him clean. When he came to Harold's chin, Harold wrapped an arm around him and pulled him close for a kiss.

"You're amazing, pup. Absolutely amazing, but I'm not done with you." He patted Taylor's hip. "Move up, pup. Brace your hands on the wall behind me and give me that dick of yours. It's my turn to taste."

Taylor moved up to straddle Harold as ordered. Harold took hold of his hips and leaned up to swallow his boy whole. He hadn't been lying when he said he wanted to taste. He sucked and bobbed his head, his mind focused on one goal: making Taylor come. He wanted to drink his boy down, and he wanted it *now*. Taylor twitched and moaned, his legs shaking against Harold's shoulders.

"Come for me, baby. I want to taste you. Come for me."

He didn't have to ask twice. With a shudder and a gasp, Taylor came. Liquid flooded Harold's mouth, and he swallowed every drop, even going so far as to return the favor by licking Taylor clean. When he was finished, he guided his boy to lie down beside him, pulling him close and wrapping his arms around him.

"Welcome home, baby."

"Thank you, Master."

Taylor was fucked. That scene with Harold had been amazing. Too amazing. His mind had latched onto the idea of Harold as his Master, and it refused to budge. Although he'd always loved pup play, he'd never wanted to belong to anyone. The play had been what mattered, so it'd been easy to arrange and enjoy scenes in the past and then move on from them. With Harold, Taylor wanted to stay.

It was official. Taylor was fucked.

In need of a distraction, he called Liam. He'd promised his ex he'd go see that apartment if it was still on the market when he got back from Florida. Might as well get that done with sooner rather than later.

"Hey, what's up?"

"I'm home," Taylor said. "Do you still want to check out that place together?"

"About that...I went already."

"You went? Alone?"

"Yeah. I mean, we met in a public place so I could make sure he wasn't an ax murderer or anything first."

Taylor rubbed his temple as he asked, "You know you can't determine if someone is an ax murderer over coffee, right?"

"I know. I got restless. And I was curious, so I went."

"And what happened?"

"I decided to take the apartment."

"That quick?"

"Taylor, if you'd seen this place, your mind would have blown. It's unreal, like something out of a movie. There's a fucking rooftop terrace with a jacuzzi. How could I resist?"

"How can you afford it?"

"He's letting me pay what I am now plus utilities."

There was no way a place with a rooftop jacuzzi would

cost so little. Liam had to be paying peanuts in comparison to this other guy. "What's the catch?" Taylor asked.

"There isn't one. He just wants to know he's not going to come home to a dusty cave."

"You're not known for keeping things clean," Taylor pointed out.

"Dust can't accumulate if someone's living in a space."

"Yes, it can. These delusions of yours about how dirt works are the reason our ceiling fan looked like it was growing mold over the edges."

"Who cleans ceiling fans?"

"Everyone," Taylor said. "Except you."

"Whatever. The bottom line is, I took the apartment."

Taylor was uneasy about the situation, but who was he to argue? As Liam's ex he wasn't sure he even had the right to be worried. "When are you moving in?"

"We're getting the paperwork squared away, and then he said I can start bringing things over. He might get called away again, so he didn't want to leave me stranded when our lease is up."

Speaking of, what date was it anyway? Taylor was startled to realize he only had two weeks left. He'd been so comfortable living at Harold's, he hadn't thought of the reality of leaving yet. He needed to start looking for a new place ASAP.

"What's this guy like, anyway?" he asked.

"He's an arrogant son of a bitch."

"And you still want to live with him?" Taylor asked incredulously.

"He's also a blond, green-eyed hunk who could manhandle me, no problem."

Given that Liam was six foot two and well-endowed

with muscles of his own, that was saying something. "You fucked him," Taylor said.

"He fucked me," Liam admitted.

"That good, huh?"

"Mind. Blown."

"Please tell me you're not staying there for the sex."

"Taylor, if you saw this apartment, you'd know that wasn't the case."

"He's not giving you a discount on the rent for that, is he?"

"Did you seriously just ask if I'm prostituting myself out for an apartment?"

"No?"

"Given the apartment, that isn't an unreasonable question," Liam said thoughtfully. "He'll be gone most of the time, though. It'd be a waste if that were his motive."

"Occasional sex is better than no sex at all," Taylor said.

"I'd still be getting the better end of the deal. Taylor, it was incredible."

"Kinky, I take it?"

"In ways I've always dreamed but never achieved before."

A pang shot through Taylor at that. It wasn't like he still wanted to be with Liam, but one of their major problems had been their inability to satisfy each other's needs. Knowing how much it went both ways still hurt.

"I'm happy for you, Liam. I hope it all works out for you."

"Thanks," Liam said. "I guess we need to schedule a date to go through the books and everything, yeah?"

"How about next weekend?"

"I'll have to check my schedule. Let's touch base during the week?"

"That works."

"Okay. And thanks. For checking in about the apartment."

"Sure."

After hanging up with Liam, Taylor called Joanne. They talked all the time, but it felt like forever since he'd seen her.

"Let's do lunch," he said when she picked up.

"You do know it's three in the afternoon, don't you?"

"I had a lazy morning."

"I bet. You sleep in Daddy's bed yet?"

"Maybe," Taylor said teasingly.

"Damn. Now I wish I could do lunch. What are you doing tomorrow?"

"Having lunch with you?"

"You bet your ass."

"See you then."

They met at Mademoiselle Crêpe. It'd been forever since Taylor had had crepes and he perused the menu with gluttonous anticipation. "I can eat three crepes for lunch, right?"

"How about you start with one and we make that decision after you finish?" Joanne suggested.

"Spoilsport."

"Are you forgetting there's a frozen yogurt place around the corner?"

"I forgive you."

After putting in their order at the counter, they found a table and sat down.

"Long time no see," Joanne said.

"I know. I'm sorry."

She waved him off. "You're in your honeymoon phase. It's natural."

"We're not married. We're not even dating."

"But you did sleep together, right?"

"I slept at the foot of his bed last night."

She paused before asking, "That counts?"

"Yes, that counts." Taylor sighed dreamily. "Especially since it was after one of the most wonderful scenes of my life."

"Details. Spill."

"He started right when I got home from the airport. I hadn't even walked in the door."

"If that were me, I'd have wanted to kill him."

"No, listen," Taylor said. "He filled up a bath for me and pet me while I soaked in it. All I had to do was unwind and not think about anything."

"The urge to kill is lessening. That sounds nice."

"He washed my hair and toweled me dry when I got out. He'd set up a mountain of blankets on the couch for me to snuggle under while he made dinner and didn't expect me to say one word through the whole thing."

"Wow," Joanne said before taking a sip of her tea. "I'm moving from annoyed into jealous. That sounds awesome. I love it when I have someone to do things for me and all I have to do is relax and enjoy the experience."

"Speaking of having someone, I heard your new contract is with Melissa."

"Yes, we are having a fantastic time playing with shibari and wax."

"That's great. How long is the contract for?"

"Three months."

"Three months?" Taylor repeated, surprised. "That's pretty long for a contract of yours."

"We're only meeting once a week, and we wanted the time to explore different ideas."

"Have you ever considered having an ongoing relationship with someone?"

Joanne leaned back in her chair and stretched her long legs in front of her. "I like my freedom too much. And I like variety."

"You could always do something poly."

"Funny enough, I couldn't," Joanne said. "My brain is designed for monogamy. I can only handle focusing on one person at a time. More than that and I'd go nuts."

"So, you focus on one person at a time in short stints instead?"

"Yup."

Taylor pursed his lips as he thought. "I can't do poly either, but I also can't do the short-term thing."

"That's not a surprise. You give your all when you care about someone, and once you've fallen it's hard for you to let go. That's why I knew you and Liam would never work out."

Taylor's brow furrowed. "How come?"

"You never fell for him. If you had, you wouldn't be walking away now. At least, not so easily."

He supposed that was true. But what did it mean for his time with Harold? He hadn't fallen for him, but he was getting attached. "I think I'm doomed."

"Cross that bridge when you come to it," Joanne said. She'd always been good at following his train of thought, even when it ran off course from where they'd started. "In the meantime, I want to hear more about last night. Please tell me there was naked time in this story. I'm long overdue one of your naked-time stories."

"Your sympathy is overwhelming."

She shifted her chair closer so she could wrap an arm around his shoulders. "You really like him?"

"I've never wanted to belong to anyone before," Taylor said. "I want to belong to him."

Joanne blew out a long, slow breath. "I don't know what to tell you, sweetie. I know you won't ask him if you can stay."

That was true. Taylor would feel like he was imposing, inviting himself into someone else's house. He couldn't do that.

"What about asking if you could continue to scene after you move out? Just because you're not living together doesn't mean everything has to stop."

"He didn't sign up for this in the first place," Taylor said. "Who says he'd want to continue? Maybe he's indulging because there's a timeline."

"Do you really believe that?"

"No." It felt unfair to Harold to think that way. "I'm afraid he'll say no. Or worse, what if he says yes but it's not the same when we're no longer living together?"

"Then you find out and deal with it. At least you'll have taken the chance."

"It's too soon to ask. I still have two weeks left."

"That's your decision, but keep it in mind, okay?"

He nodded.

A spark of hope glimmered beneath his ribs. What if he could have Harold, even if he moved out? It wouldn't be the same. He'd be back to coordinating scenes and being less spontaneous, but with Harold it might work. It could still feel like it did now, like he'd found where he belonged and was getting what he hadn't realized he needed.

Now that they'd introduced sex into their relationship, Harold had wondered how things would change between him and Taylor, but not much did. As if to counteract the intensity of their scene, the rest of the weekend had been pretty chill. They'd talked, they'd cuddled, they'd thrown popcorn at each other while watching movies. The only significant difference was Taylor slept at the foot of Harold's bed again Saturday and Sunday night.

"Are you sure you're comfortable there?" Harold asked as they were settling in for bed on Sunday.

"Yeah. I tend to sleep curled up no matter where I am."

That didn't sound like a resounding yes, but Harold didn't feel right pushing the matter. It was Taylor's choice where he wanted to sleep.

You could sleep next to me, he thought but kept from saying the words out loud. They didn't feel right. Not yet. *Oh shit. I'm imagining a future for us.*

"As long as you don't mind," he said.

"I'd rather sleep here than on the couch."

"Okay." Harold pulled the covers back and got into bed.

"Hey, Harold?"

"Yeah?"

"Could we have another date?"

"Sure. We never did go for ramen like you'd wanted. I fully expect to be wowed."

Taylor grinned. "Tomorrow night then. I'll take you to my favorite place in the city."

"It's a date."

The next day Taylor called him during his lunch break. "If we're going to have any chance of eating dinner at a decent hour, we have to leave the apartment no later than five."

"You don't get out of work until five."

"I know. That's why you're going to meet me here."

"Is that so?"

"Please?" Taylor pitched his voice in a way that made Harold picture him with those puppy dog eyes.

He sighed. "I'll meet you at your office. Where are we going anyway?"

"The Village. I'm hoping if we get there between five thirty and six the wait won't be longer than an hour."

"An hour? For ramen? What sort of place is this? Do they make the noodles out of edible gold?"

"No, but that's an interesting idea," Taylor said. "The restaurant I'm taking you to is a branch of one that exists in Japan. Joanne ate there while she was over there and took me to this one after she came back."

"Joanne went to Japan?"

"She did JET the year after she graduated college."

"What's JET?"

"It's a program where Americans can work and teach English in Japan. It'd been a dream of hers to do it."

"I had no idea she knew Japanese. You didn't go with her?"

"That was her thing."

"You like the culture enough to make me wait an hour for ramen."

"Ah, well, food is definitely one of my things, and ramen is one of my favorites. I didn't have to go to another country to learn that."

"What else are some of your things?" Harold asked, his voice softening.

There was noise in the background on Taylor's end of the line. When Taylor came back, he said, "I've got to go. Ask me again on our date."

"Will do."

A part of Harold hoped for a tour when he arrived at Taylor's workplace. The most he got to see was the lobby before Taylor grabbed his arm and whisked him away to the nearest subway station.

"Well, hello to you too," Harold said as he scrambled after him.

Once they were on the subway and it was moving, Taylor turned to him, pushing onto his toes a little to place a sweet kiss on his cheek. "Hello."

Harold's annoyance at being hustled along without any civility melted. He wrapped an arm around Taylor's waist and pulled him close. "Hello." He returned the kiss to Taylor's lips.

"You kiss on the second date?" Taylor asked.

"Seems like it."

"Do you put out?"

"Depends on how well the date goes."

Taylor pouted. "Last time the date went really well, and I got blue balled."

Harold smirked. "It's a fine line. Are you sure you're up for the challenge?"

"Ooh, I like it when you're feeling wicked."

"According to you, last time that happened you were left blue balled."

"A little denial does a boy good."

"Be careful what you wish for."

"I said 'a little.'"

Harold rolled his eyes up to the ceiling, pretending he hadn't heard.

"Just remember," Taylor said. "If I get blue balled, so do you."

Taylor's assumption of a long wait proved true. After arriving, they were informed it would be approximately forty-five minutes before they were seated, even if they chose to sit at the bar. Given the number of people crowding around the front door, this wasn't a surprise.

"All for ramen," Harold muttered under his breath.

"Told you," Taylor said.

"What are we supposed to do while we wait?"

"Don't worry. I got us covered." After giving his cell phone number to the person in charge of the waiting list, Taylor led the way back outside.

All of the benches in the waiting area had been taken and the standing room around them was filled with even more people. They went outside where there wasn't any seating, but at least there was peace, quiet, and space.

"Over here," Taylor called. He'd moved to the neighboring storefront and taken a seat on the windowsill. It was just wide enough to perch a butt cheek on if you were careful and didn't shift. "Have a seat."

"You know, you're not getting many points in the awesome date department so far," Harold said.

"Give me a chance, will you?"

"All right." Harold sat. "But I have high standards, so I'm only warning you."

"Says the man who drinks shit coffee even when good stuff is readily available."

"Coffee is fuel, not food."

"So, it's supposed to taste like gasoline?" Taylor asked.

"I drink it too fast to taste it at all," Harold admitted.

"That's unfortunate."

Concerned that Taylor had been suffering needlessly, Harold said, "You're welcome to buy something different for the apartment if it bothers you."

"I didn't mean anything by it. I was only teasing."

"I know, but you drink it as well. I'd rather you have something you like."

Taylor gave him a warm smile. "Thank you."

Harold nodded, resisting the urge to pull him closer for a kiss. Then he remembered they were on a date. Why did he have to resist? He leaned forward and pressed his lips to Taylor's. When he sat back, a light flush colored Taylor's face.

"What was that for?"

Harold shrugged. "I felt like it," he said. "Are you going to tell me why we're sitting on a window?"

"We're here because it gives us a table on which to play a game." Taylor reached into his pocket and took out a deck of cards. He pulled the cards out of the box and spread them. They were unlike anything Harold had seen before. None of the values were over ten, and the number of times each value appeared in the deck varied.

"Are you trying to cheat me?"

Taylor laughed. "No, this is the way the deck is supposed to look. Have you ever heard of the game Pairs?"

"No."

"You have now. And I'm going to teach you one of the many ways to play it."

Half an hour later, Harold was absorbed in the game. He was disappointed when Taylor's cell phone rang and they were informed their table was ready.

"We can play more when we get home," Taylor said.

"Definitely. You just got ahead of me by one point. There's no way I'm leaving things as they are."

Taylor laughed.

They headed into the restaurant and were seated at a table for two among the crowd. It wasn't the most ideal atmosphere for a date in Harold's opinion, but one look at Taylor across the way and he didn't mind at all.

The waiter handed them each a one-page menu and left them alone. Harold looked the menu over and saw words he'd never heard of before. *Shoyu, tonkotsu, chashu...*

"I didn't realize there was so much to ramen."

Taylor grinned. "Told you."

"What do you recommend?"

"How hungry are you?"

"Hungry enough," Harold said. "Why?"

"I was thinking you should get the *shoyu*, and I'll get the *tonkotsu*, and when we're done, we can get a refill of noodles and trade."

"That sounds like a lot of noodles."

"I did ask if you were hungry. Are you up for it?"

Harold smiled. "Absolutely."

He let Taylor order, not wanting to massacre the words, and when they were alone again, Taylor asked, "Are you impressed yet?"

"I'll give you intrigued. I can't be impressed until I've tasted everything."

"I'm not worried."

"So confident. What else do you have planned for the evening?"

"Why are you in such a rush?" Taylor asked. "Let's take one experience at a time."

"I was wondering how fast we'll be home so I can kick your ass at cards."

"You're that hung up on one point?"

Harold leaned forward, looking into Taylor's milk chocolate brown eyes. "I'm competitive."

Taylor mirrored his position. "Maybe we should make things interesting then."

"What did you have in mind?"

"A little wager?"

"Stakes?"

"If I win…" Taylor bit his lip and let it roll out slowly. "I want to kiss you."

"That's a waste," Harold said. "You can do that now."

"I didn't say where."

Oh, the possibilities. "And if I win?"

"What do you want?"

Right now, Harold really wanted to know where Taylor planned to kiss him. "If I win, you do the laundry, start to finish, wearing nothing but your G-string." He saw Taylor's pupils dilate and smiled. "Deal?"

Taylor's grin matched his own. "Deal."

Harold was looking forward to their game no matter the outcome.

The waiter arrived with two giant bowls of what he assumed was ramen. When he looked inside the bowl placed in front of him, he saw the broth and noodles he expected along with a lot more. Pork slices, seaweed, bamboo shoots, and something white with a pink swirl in it. Never one to shy from new food experiences, he picked up his chopsticks and took a taste.

"This is delicious," he said.

"See? I told you."

"You were right."

"I love a man who can admit when he's wrong."

"Is that so?"

"Yes," Taylor said, "it's one of the most attractive attributes after a good sense of humor, the ability to cook, and a great ass."

"I'm partial to a great ass myself."

"Good thing I've been blessed with one."

"It is one of your finer attributes."

"But not my only fine attribute."

"No, definitely not the only one," Harold agreed. "I do have a weakness for those puppy dog eyes of yours." Even now, Harold couldn't help but be lost in them. He reached across the table and caressed Taylor's cheek.

Taylor licked his lips. "Maybe we'll take that second helping of noodles to go."

"We still need to finish the first," Harold pointed out. He took another bite of his dinner. It really was good. It was actually a meal, unlike the instant things he'd had in college. "What other delicious food secrets do you know?"

"This isn't exactly a secret," Taylor said, gesturing to the crowd around them.

"It was a secret to me."

"I wonder what other food pleasures you've been deprived of."

"We'll have to find out so you can introduce me to them. You did say food was one of your things."

Taylor's smile was soft. "I did."

"You should design a food tour for us. Each day we'll eat a different food. Or we can save it for weekends and do lunch instead of dinner." As soon as the words left his mouth, he regretted them. He only had one more weekend left with Taylor. "Dinner's fine," he said.

Taylor's smile faded. "We'll figure it out."

Harold nodded and they resumed eating, but the knowledge of their limited time together tainted the atmosphere. They ended up ordering their extra noodles to go and took their leftovers home. The mood lifted as they entered the apartment, as if the space were some alternate universe untouched by time or outside obligation.

"We have a card game to finish," Taylor announced.

"Yes, we do. Prepare to have that fine ass of yours handed to you."

Taylor laughed.

They arranged themselves around the coffee table, trading their bowls of ramen like Taylor had suggested. Harold grabbed a few beers from the fridge, and Taylor took the cards out of his pocket and dealt.

"You didn't cheat while I wasn't looking, did you?" Harold asked as he sat down.

"Oh no. I'm going to win fair and square. I want that kiss."

"If you're lucky, maybe I'll let you have it after you're done with the laundry."

"Keep dreaming, Grandpa. That's a fantasy you'll have to work for another day."

"Grandpa, is it?" Harold said, raising an eyebrow. "We're bringing in the age gap now?"

"It's all part of my strategy to psych you out."

"I have news for you, kid. I'm getting the better end of this deal. Bringing up my age is only going to make me preen." He was preening as he said it.

"You're not afraid someone's going to think you're my father when they see us together?"

"I'll tell them you call me Daddy with a capital *D*."

"I do not!"

"They don't know that. Maybe they'll think I spank you when you're naughty."

Taylor squirmed. "You *should* spank me when I'm naughty."

Well, this conversation took a turn. "Is that so?"

"Come on, Daddy. Don't you want to give it to your boy?"

"What happened to not calling me Daddy?"

Taylor leaned forward and crawled to Harold's side of the table. He looked up and licked his lips. "Please, Master," he said, "won't you spank your pup?"

Oh fuck. "If this is a ploy to look at my cards, you won't enjoy the spanking."

Taylor grinned, but before he could say anything, Harold grabbed the front of his shirt and hauled him closer for a kiss. Taylor opened his mouth, welcoming Harold's hungry invasion. Following Harold's urging, he crawled into Harold's lap, pressing their bodies together. The proximity brought friction and warmth and accessibility to their kiss. Harold wrapped his arms around his pup and lost himself in the moment. By the time their lips parted, they were panting.

"I'm still going to win this card game," Harold declared breathlessly.

"Whatever you say, not-Daddy."

With a growl, Harold fumbled Taylor's pants open. He yanked the seat down, exposing Taylor's perfectly firm ass, and spanked one of the cheeks. Taylor cried out in surprise, then knelt up to allow for easier access.

"Again. Please!" he begged.

Harold obliged, holding Taylor firmly against him with one hand while he reddened his butt with the other. Taylor dug his fingers into Harold's shoulders, rocking his hips as he cried out "Again!" after each strike. Harold's palm began to tingle, and he would have worried it was too much if Taylor hadn't been so eager for it.

"One more!"

Harold spanked him.

"One more!"

He did it again

"So close! One more!"

It took three more and suddenly Taylor was coming, his hips jerking against Harold's chest. When he finished, he hung like a monkey, his arms wrapped around Harold's neck.

"Good?"

Taylor nodded.

"You left a wet spot on my shirt."

Taylor laughed. "Want me to lick it clean?"

"No need."

"Want me to lick anything else?"

Tempting as the offer was, Harold said, "Let's finish the game first. I can always fuck you before you do the laundry."

"Still so confident."

"You can wear the G-string and my cum."

"Technically, that's changing the stakes," Taylor said as he made his way back to the other side of the table. He hadn't bothered to pull his pants up and Harold could see how red his rear end was.

"Are you all right?" he asked.

"Huh? Oh. I'm fine. I'll put lotion on it before bed to soothe the sting. It'll be a little sore tomorrow, but it's nothing problematic." Taylor smiled. "It'll be a nice distraction when I'm bored at work."

As long as he hadn't gone too far. "Are you sure you don't want me to do that for you now?" Harold asked.

"Nah. I want to kick your butt at cards first." Taylor grinned.

"Is that so?" Harold grabbed one of the softer pillows from the couch and tossed it at him.

"Thank you," Taylor said. He removed his pants before sitting on it.

"Trying to psych me out again?"

"I don't want the fabric rubbing. My skin's a bit sensitive at the moment." He glanced down at his naked lower half. "But the distraction possibilities are a nice bonus."

Harold shook his head and picked up his cards. "Let's play."

Taylor ended up winning. Harold was disappointed, but he couldn't feel too bad about it. He was sure the kiss Taylor had in mind would be a prize for both of them.

"Why haven't we done this earlier?" he asked as they cleaned up.

Taylor shrugged. "I don't know. I never thought of it."

"Do you play other games?"

"Oh yeah. There's a whole shelf full back at my place. I could bring some over if you want."

It might be nice to play a game sometimes instead of letting Netflix be their main source of entertainment. "Do it," Harold said. "I need the opportunity for a rematch."

Taylor smirked. "Be careful what you wish for."

Chapter Twelve

An overwhelming workweek kept Taylor from cashing in his winnings from the bet until Thursday. After dinner that night, when they'd both taken showers, instead of settling on the couch as usual, Taylor asked Harold to lie down in the bedroom. The sight of the man laid out naked before him was like a holiday feast, and Taylor was eager to partake. He trailed a hand down Harold's back, the skin pale from lack of sun, and followed the curve to where it rose into the round globes of Harold's backside. They weren't as firm as they must have been when he'd been Taylor's age, but they still looked good enough to eat. Luckily for Taylor, that was the reward he was owed for their bet.

"Can you spread your legs for me?"

Harold obliged, and Taylor leaned over from the foot of the bed to settle between them. Harold smelled clean and inviting. He palmed the man's ass, taking a moment to savor the anticipation. He'd wanted to do this for a long time and wasn't going to rush.

Taylor spread Harold's cheeks so he could place the kiss

he'd won between them. He made lazy circles with his tongue around Harold's hole before pressing against the tight muscles, coaxing them to soften.

Harold groaned as he teased the intimate skin. "That feels good."

Taylor was glad. He wanted Harold to enjoy himself.

As he continued, his body inevitably produced its own response, but he ignored it. His desire right now was for something more than an orgasm, something epic but intangible. Doing this for Harold without expecting anything in return fed a part of him that went deeper than sex. It was an extension of his pup play kink, but instead of fulfilling a need for himself, it awakened a desire in him to give, to share, to serve.

Taylor had never felt this way before. He'd never thought to try for it either because he'd never had a Master to serve. Any Master he'd played with had been temporary or borrowed, never his. Even though their time together was still temporary, Harold was different from the others. This meant something with him.

Taylor lost himself to his task. When Harold's movements and sounds became more urgent, he realized his tongue was aching and his lips tingled. He wouldn't be able to continue much longer. Thankfully, Harold shifted to the side so he could reach a hand beneath his body and began to jerk off.

"Stick it in," he ordered.

Taylor did, shaping the tip of his tongue into a point and pressing it forward. Harold let out an agonized groan, and, after a few more moments, shuddered his release. Taylor waited where he was for his Master to recover. Eventually, Harold waved a hand, indicating Taylor should move up beside him. He pulled Taylor close once he was in reach.

"That was the kiss you wanted?"

"Yes."

"Happy with your winnings?"

"Very."

Harold wrapped his arms around him. "You're sleeping with me tonight."

He'd been sleeping at the foot of Harold's bed all week. "You mean like this?" Taylor asked.

Harold nodded. "Beside me."

"Okay. But can we move under the covers? I'm going to freeze if we stay this way."

"You don't think I can keep you warm?" Harold teased as they maneuvered the sheet and blankets over them.

"I have full confidence in your abilities as long as you have blanket assistance."

"If I wasn't worn out from a fantastic orgasm, I'd give you a scathing reply."

"I'll pretend I'm suitably wounded."

"Thank you."

It was really nice drifting off to sleep next to Harold. His body provided extra warmth against Taylor's back as they spooned, and his arms made Taylor feel safe and secure.

I could fall in love with sleeping like this.

***

The next morning Liam called while Taylor was on his way to work.

"Do you have time to sort the apartment this weekend?" he asked.

"I should have some time tomorrow." Harold was

meeting with James and some of his associates. If things went well, it could lead to more clients for his work.

"Ten?" Liam asked.

"Sure."

Wait a minute, what date was it? Taylor reunlocked his phone and checked. Holy shit. Their lease was up in a week. He'd meant to start looking for an apartment last weekend, but work had kicked his ass, and he'd forgotten all about it. Work and the allure of being with Harold.

During his lunch break he did a quick search for available apartments, but the looming deadline made him too anxious to concentrate. After making a few notes, he gave up and focused on his job. He'd have time to look during the weekend. He'd buckle down and figure it all out then.

The following morning, he met Liam at their apartment. Unlike the last time he'd been there, Liam's stuff wasn't all over the place. In fact, it looked like most of it was gone.

"Are you sure you haven't moved out already?" Taylor asked.

"All my clothes, toiletries, and bedding are at Damian's place. I moved everything in batches over the past week."

Taylor hadn't even begun to think about the logistics of moving. He needed boxes, a plan. As the weekend's to-do list compounded in his mind, so did the weight pressing down on him. *Too much. Too much! Too much!* He forced himself to focus on the task at hand. "All we need to go through is the media and books?"

Liam nodded. "That was our mutual collection."

Taylor looked at the overstuffed bookcase. "We should get started. We're going to be here a while."

Three hours later they paused for a lunch break.

"You're really sure about moving in with this guy?" Taylor asked before taking a bite of his biryani.

"You're still worried?"

"The situation is strange."

"Aren't you living with some guy you just met?"

"He didn't put out an online ad to lure me in."

Liam laughed. "You don't have to worry, Taylor. I'm fine."

"Can't help it. Just because we're not dating anymore doesn't mean I don't care."

"I appreciate that," Liam said. "Which brings us to the 'can we still be friends' crossroads conversation."

"Crossroads conversation?"

"The crossroads is the question of if we have the conversation or not."

"Do you want to?" Taylor asked.

"We are a part of the same community and have a lot of friends and acquaintances in common."

"We can be civil whether we remain friends or not. Look at us right now," Taylor pointed out. "I think the choice of remaining friends doesn't depend on our environment. It depends on us."

"So what do you think?"

"I asked you first."

They looked at each other, and Taylor wondered if they were both hesitating to admit the truth: they weren't going to remain friends.

"How about time will tell?" Liam suggested.

"Leave it up to fate?"

"Leave it up to the natural course of life."

This really was an ending. Taylor could feel it. Although he wouldn't change anything, he was still a little sad about it.

"We'll leave it up to chance," he said.

Harold came home from lunch in a good mood. James had a varied group of acquaintances, which had made for a very interesting meal. He was reasonably confident at least a few of the people he'd met would call him for work.

He entered the apartment to find Taylor at the breakfast bar, his attention absorbed in his laptop and a notepad by his side. On the notepad was a list of addresses, building notes, and pricing.

He's looking for an apartment.

It shouldn't have come as a shock, but it did. They only had a week before Taylor moved out. Somehow Harold had thought that day would never come. That Taylor would always be living with him.

"I'm going to pick up Chinese for dinner and bring it back. Do you want anything?"

Taylor glanced up from the screen. "You just got home. Why not order delivery?"

Harold shrugged. "I don't feel like waiting, and I still have my coat on."

"Okay. I'll have my usual and an extra order of fried wontons."

"Got it. I'll be back in a few." He turned and headed out. Once outside, he took a deep breath, inhaling the stench of garbage left out for pickup in the morning. He gagged, coughed, and moved to fresher air. The trash was a pile of black bags, no giant cardboard boxes with unconscious beautiful men inside.

I can't believe it's been four weeks already. It was too fast, too soon. Their deadline couldn't be up yet.

He pulled out his phone and dialed his sister's number.

"What's up, baby bro?"

He took another deep breath, thankfully successfully this time. "Taylor's lease is up on Friday."

"And you don't want him to go." She didn't even make it a question. There was no reason to. They'd both known it would happen.

"What do I do?" he asked.

"Why not ask him to stay? He might be as reluctant to leave as you are to have him go."

"I'm afraid of him saying no."

"Do you think that's likely?"

"It's the possibility that's making me hesitate."

"And how much of a possibility is there? You've been living together for four weeks now. People learn more about each other after they've moved in together than they do from six months of dating. Do you really think he's going to say no?"

"We never talked about it, so I really don't know."

"Let me ask you this—even if he moves out, do you think whatever you have will end?"

"I don't want it to."

"And him?"

Harold thought of all the times Taylor had called him Master and the way he'd said the word. "No, I don't think he wants it to either."

"Then talk to him, little brother. Find out what you have together and how you can make it work before you run out of time."

She was right. "I will."

"Good. Love you."

"Love you, too."

He was feeling marginally better by the time he got the

food and came back home. He wouldn't be completely settled until he'd had that talk with Taylor, but now wasn't the right time. His pup was too absorbed in his task. Instead, he put on a brave face and joined Taylor at the breakfast bar.

"Find anything?" he asked.

"No." Taylor sat back and rubbed his hands over his face. "I should have started this search a lot earlier. How am I going to find a place in a weekend? I'm never going to be able to afford an apartment on my own, not unless I want to be ridiculously far from work, but how can I live with someone I barely know?" He sighed. "And it isn't just the apartment. I need to figure out how I'm packing up all my stuff and moving it." His face contorted like he was about to cry. "It's my own fault. I know that. I procrastinated and didn't think about it, and now I've gotten myself into this mess, but it's all just..."

Harold wrapped an arm around him and pulled him to his side. "Stop." He pressed a kiss against Taylor's temple. "Take a minute and breathe. You're going to be fine."

Taylor let out a long, shuddering breath. "I know. I'm just overwhelmed."

"We'll work through it one step at a time so you won't stay that way." He pulled back so he could look at Taylor. "First off, how about we ease your deadline? If you need to stay here a little longer, that's fine. I'm not going to kick you out."

Taylor's eyes were still haunted, but the wildness in them receded. "Thank you," he said.

"Do you think you can take your mind off of it for a while? Maybe take a break and eat those extra wontons?"

Taylor shook his head. "Not yet. I can't relax yet."

"Okay." Harold reached into the takeout bag and pulled

out a package of fried wontons. "I'm going to get a plate so you can snack on these while you search. In a couple of hours, we'll have dinner."

Taylor smiled, looking steadier than before. "That sounds like a great idea."

"Good." Harold kissed the top of his head. "I'll leave you to it then. Might as well get some work done while you're searching. Otherwise, I'll be tempted to distract you."

"Am I that irresistible?" Taylor teased, and Harold knew his anxiety had subsided.

"Fiendishly so."

"Mmm...I'm finding myself distracted."

"Oh no," Harold said. "Back to your computer. Search now, play later."

"Frisbee?"

"Not tonight. It'll be too late by the time we finish dinner. We can go tomorrow, but only if you get to work and stop procrastinating."

Taylor pouted. "Yes, Master."

"Bratty pup."

Taylor grinned and Harold went to get his own laptop.

Taylor wasn't sure how much time passed before Harold called him to the coffee table for dinner. Unease still plagued him, but it was more of a background hum for the time being than a devastating symphony. Being able to stay longer at Harold's had gone a long way to settling his nerves.

It had also been a disappointment.

He was truly grateful for what Harold was offering him, but not kicking him out wasn't the same as asking him to stay. If Harold was going to do one of those things, Taylor wanted the latter.

This whole ordeal would be over and done with if you asked me to stay.

That wasn't fair to Harold, though. It wasn't his fault Taylor was in this situation, and he'd been kind enough to let Taylor move in at all.

But if there was going to be any possibility of them living together permanently, Harold would have to be the one to suggest it. Taylor couldn't insist on staying longer. His mind rebelled at the thought of imposing on someone else's space, and moving in counted as the biggest of impositions.

Even if Taylor couldn't be Harold's permanent roommate, he would ask to still see him. Losing his place in Harold's apartment was one thing, but he couldn't lose Harold entirely. Not when they'd come so far. No matter what, he'd find a way to keep this connection they'd found.

"Have you thought about packing?" Harold asked.

"That was on my list after finding an apartment."

"Might want to move it up a bit."

He was right. "After dinner I'll call Joanne and see if I can store some stuff at her place."

"How big is her place?"

"Big, but not big enough."

"What about getting a storage unit?" Harold asked as he doled noodles onto a plate and handed it over. "You can rent it for a month and not have to worry."

"How much do those things cost?"

"Depends on the size. How much furniture are you moving?"

Oh shit. Suddenly there was a lot more to move than he'd thought.

Something must have shown on his face because Harold put a hand on his shoulder. "Look, why don't we stop by your apartment tomorrow and see how much stuff there is to move? Then we can decide how big of a unit you'll need and go from there."

Taylor nodded. What would he have done without Harold?

"You have a week to move everything, right? Call Joanne after dinner and see if you can leave some of the smaller things at her place. You can also bring some here. We'll see what we can move when we're at the apartment tomorrow and do the rest in batches during the week."

"How are we going to move the furniture? We'll have to rent a truck."

"It so happens I have a friend on Long Island with a pickup. Depending on what you have to move, we may not need more than that."

Taylor scooted closer to Harold on the couch and nuzzled him. "Thank you," he said.

"Hey, what are Masters for?"

When Harold woke the next morning, Taylor was already back at his computer looking for apartments. He didn't know what time his pup had risen, but he gave him a solid two hours before calling for a break.

"Get showered and dressed. We're going for a walk and then we'll have lunch."

Taylor went to do as bid without a word of complaint. Despite getting up at god knew what hour, he looked a lot better than yesterday. Harold was relieved. He'd hated the look on his pup's face last night when he'd been anxious about the move.

If you asked him to stay, he wouldn't have to stress at all.

But that was only if he said yes. What if he said no?

Then he might feel trapped having to stay longer with me, which would only be more stressful.

"Any luck?" Harold asked when Taylor emerged from the bathroom twenty minutes later.

"Maybe. I found someone whose lease is renewing in June who's in need of a roommate. The location's great, and the apartment looks good, but I don't know if they've found someone already. I emailed them to find out."

"That's a good start," Harold said.

It was another beautiful day for a walk, but this time the crowd was thick enough to squash their plan to play Frisbee. Instead, they meandered, enjoying the sunshine and each other's company. It was peaceful, especially when Taylor reached for him, and they walked hand in hand.

For lunch they went to Ceres, a small Italian restaurant on the way to Taylor's apartment. It was a little hole-in-the-wall place with delicious food. They lingered longer than they should have, overstuffing themselves with extra servings of warm garlic bread.

When they finally motivated themselves to continue on, Harold guided them to a store where they could pick up packing boxes, and Taylor called Joanne to let her know they were on the way. When he'd spoken with her the night before, she'd agreed to help them pack.

"Are we going to bump into Liam?" Harold asked as they neared the apartment.

"No, he's pretty much moved into his new place."

"The sketchy one?"

"Yup."

"He really went for it?" Harold asked, surprised.

"Apparently, his future roommate isn't as disreputable as his ad suggests."

"Oh?"

"He's also hot and really good in bed."

"Ah."

Harold wasn't sure what he'd been expecting when he entered Taylor's place, but it wasn't the unbalanced, semi-lifeless atmosphere he found. Taylor hadn't been exaggerating when he'd said Liam had already moved out. The empty places that someone used to fill made the room feel off-kilter. As he looked around, he realized it was more than half-empty. The books, Blu-rays, and DVDs were stacked next to the bookcase he assumed they used to belong in, and Taylor's clothes were already at his place.

"Where do you want to start?" he asked. "Taylor?"

"Huh? Oh. Sorry. I drifted off."

"That's okay. I said where do you want to start?"

Taylor looked around the room again. "There's less here than I thought there would be."

"I'm sure it's more than you think."

Taylor nodded. "The kitchen's going to be an adventure," he said distractedly. "I don't think Liam took anything from there."

Harold moved closer and put an arm around him. "Are you all right?"

"Yeah, I just...I kind of knew it, but it didn't really sink in before."

"What?"

"Liam's not the only one who's already moved out."

The urge rose, irresistible like an eruption. "Taylor, would you want—"

His sentence was cut off by a knock on the door.

"That'll be Joanne." Taylor went to answer it.

"Sorry I'm late," Joanne said as she entered, patting stray drops of water from her jeans and shirt. "There was a sudden sun shower, and I had to hide under an awning to miss the brunt of it."

"You're not late," Taylor assured here. "We just got here too."

"Oh good. So what's the plan? Hi, Harold." She flashed a bright smile his way.

"Hi, Joanne."

"I don't know," Taylor said.

"Why don't you look over the bedroom, Taylor?" Harold suggested. "Joanne can finish up the stray things in here, and I'll get a head start on the kitchen."

Joanne shrugged. "Sounds like as good a plan as any."

They broke up into their respective rooms and got to work.

"We need a soundtrack or something," Joanne called out ten minutes later. "This is boring."

Harold could hear Taylor sigh in the bedroom. "It would be more motivating."

"Oh! Yes!" Joanne exclaimed.

"What?"

She didn't reply, but a few minutes later music filtered down the hallway from the living room. "I found your shower speaker," she explained. "Why wasn't it in the bathroom?"

"It's not specifically for the shower. That's just the reason I bought it."

"Well, thankfully we didn't have to wait for someone to sort the bathroom to find it."

"What are we listening to?" Harold asked.

There were gasps from the rooms on either side of him.

"Harold, Harold, Harold," Joanne said. "I will forgive you that question by attributing it to the generation gap."

"I'm trying extremely hard not to be insulted right now," Harold said.

"I didn't mean to insult you, Daddy." Her voice was coy, and he laughed.

"I take it they're popular?"

"Extremely," said Taylor. "Or they were. They've broken up by now."

"Okay, I'm updating my playlist," Joanne said. "Harold, we will now introduce you to all of Taylor's and my favorites."

"Only if I can return the favor."

There was a momentary pause before she said, "I suppose that's only fair."

"Don't sound so reluctant. What do you think I'm going to subject you to?"

"I have no idea. When you were forming your musical tastes, we weren't even a thought on our parents' radar."

"Musical tastes are formed in our early teens. How old do you think I am?"

"Forty?" she ventured.

"Yes! We're separated by a decade, not a century."

"Isn't it crazy," Taylor interjected, "that people only six years younger than us were born in a different century? Not only that, they were born in a different millennium."

Silence followed his statement.

"Now I feel old," Joanne said.

"Good," Harold said.

They let the pop music play and continued working. After an hour, Harold took over the playlist and to Joanne's surprise, she liked his taste more than she'd anticipated.

"Crap. How are we going to move all of this to your apartments?" Taylor asked when they were nearing the end of their packing.

"I told you I'd call a friend of mine to help us," Harold said.

"How come I haven't met any of your friends?" Taylor asked.

"Wondering if I really have any?"

"Maybe."

"I do. This one's name is Kossi, and he's a friend from college. He lives on Long Island, so we only get to see each other for the occasional dinner."

"And he would be willing to drive into the city to help out?"

"He will once I offer to buy dinner next time."

"That's not even going to cover the gas it'll take to get here."

"It will when it's a lobster dinner."

"Oh."

"Yeah."

"But..." Taylor still felt bad making Harold's friend drive all the way from Long Island. "He really doesn't mind?"

"Minimum weight for the lobster is three pounds. He won't mind at all."

"Speaking of dinner," Joanne said, "I'm starving. Think delivery will get here before your friend?"

"It's a chance I'm willing to take."

"Thai?"

"Sounds good to me."

"I'll call," Joanne volunteered. "Beef satay and spicy basil chicken, right, Taylor?"

"Yes, please."

"I'll have the same," Harold said.

She went into the other room to make the phone call, and Taylor took the opportunity to pull Harold aside.

"Thank you," he said.

"I offered to help."

"I meant calling your friend. You didn't sign up to pay someone a lobster dinner to help me."

Harold ran a hand through Taylor's hair. "I'm happy to help, pup." He kissed

Taylor's temple. "We'll move the furniture during the week, but is there anything you want to take now besides the boxes? The TV maybe?"

The TV had been his, though all the game systems had gone with Liam. "How much can we fit in your friend's car?"

"It's a pickup truck. We'll be fine."

"Let's take the TV then."

"Food's on the way," Joanne announced as she reentered the room.

"Let's stack everything in the living room while we wait," Harold suggested.

"Oh, I meant to tell you," Joanne said to Taylor when they were fetching the last boxes from the bedroom. "There's a party tonight. Want me to send you the details?"

"I don't have the brain power to think about that right now."

"Might as well. You're all packed up and we're clearing the bulk of your stuff out of here today. You've got feelers out for a new apartment, and Harold already said he won't rush you if you need to stay longer. You're in a good place. Take a moment to dump the stress."

"It's Sunday. I don't know if Harold would go out on a work night."

"The man works from home and for himself. He can adjust his hours if he wants to sleep in tomorrow."

Taylor was still indecisive.

"Doesn't hurt to ask." She put a hand on his shoulder. "You've done the adulting. You're allowed to have fun, Taylor."

"Let's get this all sorted and then I'll think about it."

"I'll text you the details just in case."

"Okay."

***

Harold's friend was generally nice, but Taylor didn't get a chance to really get to know him. As soon as he arrived, he and Harold took charge of puzzling the boxes into the bed of the truck in a way nothing would get lost or damaged. Taylor and Joanne left them to it.

"We can't all fit into the truck," Joanne said.

"Maybe you should head to your place first so you can open the door for them when they get there?"

"You're making me travel on my own?"

"You came here on your own."

"But now we're all going to the same place from the same place." She fanned herself as if trying to keep from crying. "I knew it. You found a man and now you're going to abandon me." She held a hand up when he opened his mouth to object. "No. I see how it is. Best friends get tossed aside when there's good sex and kink to be had. And here I'd assumed our friendship would stand the test of time."

"Are you done?"

She tilted her head thoughtfully. "I'm not sure."

"Let me cut you off before you decide. I'll take the subway with you."

"Don't go doing me any favors."

"Guess you weren't done being contrary."

"Are you sure you want to leave them alone in the truck together? That friend of Harold's is kind of hot."

"Joanne!"

She grinned. "Let your Master know we're heading off and we'll meet them. They look like they're almost done, and we need to get a head start."

Taylor did as instructed and was surprised when Harold pulled him close for a quick kiss before sending him off with a "Be careful, pup." He was flushed and still shocked when they descended the stairs into the subway.

"Did you see that?" he asked Joanne.

"Yup."

"It was like I was his boyfriend."

"Maybe he wants to be your boyfriend."

"If that were true, I wish he'd tell me."

"You really won't consider asking if you could stay permanently?"

Taylor sighed. "You know I can't do that. The thought of imposing makes my blood freeze."

"What if you...didn't ask? What if you suggested the idea to him in a way that hinted you wouldn't say no if he asked?"

"How the hell am I supposed to do that?"

"Hey, I only come up with brilliant ideas. It's up to you to figure out the execution."

"Your desire to help is astounding," Taylor said. "Saintly."

Joanne preened as if he hadn't been sarcastic. "I know."

They arrived before Harold and Kossi and helped to unload some of the boxes into Joanne's apartment. Then Taylor squeezed into the truck with the men, and they were off to Harold's. On the way, Taylor received a text from Joanne.

Joanne: Don't forget about the party!

A second message had the details she'd promised to send him.

At Harold's, they stacked the remaining boxes against the wall and on the dining room table. As soon as they were finished, Kossi said a quick goodbye and headed off.

"He really only came to help?"

"Yes."

"I feel like we wasted a lot of his time."

"Joanne came to help. You don't feel bad about that."

"She's my friend. She knows me. And she also didn't drive an hour to get here for fifteen minutes of assistance."

"Are you bad at accepting help from people?"

"From strangers, yes."

Harold looked at him and waited.

"And from friends when I haven't asked for it," he admitted.

Harold stepped closer and pulled him into a hug. "What will make you feel better?"

Taylor sank into the hug. "I don't know." After a moment he added, "This is good."

Harold laughed and hugged him tighter. "What did you want to do tonight?"

Taylor's phone chimed before he could answer. He reluctantly pulled out of Harold's embrace so he could check it. It was a Facebook message from his potential room-mate. He opened the app and scanned the contents. A smile spread across his face as he read the message a second time.

"They still have the room for rent!"

"What?"

"The apartment I told you about. The room is still avail-able, and they want to meet so we can see if we want to live together."

"That's...great."

It was. The weight Taylor had been carrying around the past few days lifted from his shoulders. It might not work out with this person, but he finally felt like he was getting somewhere. He quickly wrote back asking if he could meet them on his lunch break tomorrow or after he finished work. They responded that tomorrow afternoon was better, and they set the time for two.

"I feel so much better now," he said. He felt amazing, like everything would be all right. It made him want to treat himself. He looked up at Harold. "Do you want to go to a pup play party tonight?"

Chapter Thirteen

Harold was internally panicking. *He's leaving. Stop him! Stop him!* He needed to ask Taylor to stay. Now, before he signed a new lease and it became too late. He'd just opened his mouth to say something, anything, when Taylor asked, "Do you want to go to a pup play party tonight?" halting his thoughts in their tracks.

"What?"

"I know it's totally last minute, but Joanne mentioned it earlier."

This was not the conversation he'd been desperate to have seconds ago. "I'm not really sure what that means, Taylor."

"Yes, you do. It's a house party, but everyone there is kinky. And the kink is the same as what we've been doing all this time."

Kinky. Harold glanced down at his slacks and plain clothing. "I'm not sure I'd fit in."

"Are you kidding? You'd be the hottest Master there. And you don't have to wear anything special. You could go in jeans and a black T-shirt. You'll be fine."

Taylor obviously wanted to go. Excitement had him rocking on his heels as he waited for Harold's answer.

Who am I kidding? I can't say no to him.

"How would this work?" he asked. "With us? With"—he waved a hand around—"the party?"

"Well..." Taylor ducked his head shyly and bit his lip. "You'd go as my Master. Would that be okay?"

If Taylor thought Harold could go to a party and let other people fawn all over his pup, he didn't know him at all. "Good," he said.

Taylor smiled and the brightness in his eyes returned. "There's probably going to be a room where the pups get to play together, similar to what I do here. There will also be people doing scenes around the place, different kinds. We don't have to do anything you don't want to. We can just go and hang out. Talk to people and maybe watch a couple of scenes."

Harold could handle that. "Joanne's going as well?" It would make him feel better if Taylor wasn't the only person he knew at the place.

"Yeah. I'll text her to find out what time she's planning on leaving so we can meet up with her there."

"Joanne does pup play?"

"She does kitty play sometimes."

"Kitty play?"

"Instead of a dog, the submissive is a cat."

"Last I heard, cats weren't ones for taking orders."

Taylor shrugged. "Maybe that's part of the appeal."

For others, but not for Taylor. And not for Harold either. "Okay. We can go."

Harold was still worried about being out of place, even though Taylor had said jeans and a T-shirt would be fine. It didn't help that Taylor had gone full pup with his mask hidden under his jacket and sweats covering his G-string. It was the same outfit Harold had originally found him in, except this time he was wearing the kneepads Harold had bought for him.

"How do I look?" he'd asked before covering up with the sweatpants.

"You look like a walking temptation. The only thing that's missing is a tail."

Taylor grinned. "That's not the only thing that's missing."

Harold had furrowed his brows in confusion, but Taylor hadn't elaborated. He was still wondering what the comment had meant when they arrived at the party.

The house was a simple mustard-yellow split-level with big windows and an array of landscaped bushes covering the front lawn. The only space free of greenery was the driveway and the stone walk to the front door. It stood like an independent rebel among a crowd of identical two-story buildings in beige, taupe, and gray. Music thumped from inside, but the windows were empty.

"Do they play in the dark?" Harold asked as they crunched their way up the gravel driveway.

"The windows are blocked with heavy curtains."

Of course. He should have guessed.

They were greeted at the door by an androgenous-looking person who ushered them inside. Harold assumed they were the host as they said, "Excess clothing can be left in the room at the top of the stairs. First floor is food, drinks, and general mingling. Downstairs is the pup room and the dungeon. Have fun!" After delivering their speech, they vanished among the partygoers.

Harold wasn't sure what he'd been expecting. At first glance it looked like every other house party he'd never been to. The entryway opened straight into the living room where random people milled in small groups, talking, holding drinks, and eating off little plates of hors d'oeuvres. To the left was an open archway and the dining room. A buffet of finger foods was set up on the dining room table. Mellow music filtered through speakers installed at various points where the walls met the ceiling. It didn't match the driving bass he'd heard outside, which he found curious, but it allowed for conversation without screaming.

Overall, the setup was pretty ordinary, if a little upscale for Harold's taste. It was the people who were unusual. Quite a few were standing around, but a bunch of them were kneeling. Many of the pups were in varying states of undress, so Taylor's G-string wouldn't stand out. Where he did see clothing, he saw mostly black and a lot of leather. There were a few dashes of red and one eye-catching pair of pants in electric blue. He wasn't the only one in jeans, though, which made him feel marginally better. Maybe it wouldn't be as obvious that he didn't fit in.

Besides the general mingling, owners fed their pups appetizers by hand. Other pups were drinking out of water bowls like the one he'd bought for Taylor. Most of the pups had collars, and some were on leashes held by their Masters or Mistresses. *Could that be what Taylor had been referring to? Did he want a collar?* Some pups also had mittens that looked like paws. One was covered from head to toe like Harold had seen online. Yet despite the unusual wardrobe and activity, it was all very calm and casual. The tension Harold had been carrying since Taylor mentioned the party abated a little more. He wasn't as far out of his depth as he'd feared. He might be able to pretend he belonged here.

"There you are!" Joanne exclaimed, weaving her way out of the crowd. A cute brunette followed behind her. She didn't have much choice since Joanne had a leash in hand that led to a thick collar around the girl's throat. She was also wearing cat ears and he could see a long tail curling up behind her. He assumed the unknown woman was Melissa. "I was wondering if you'd make it."

"We made it," Taylor said as he shed his sweatpants. "I told you we would make it."

"I'm so glad. Besides Larry, I barely know anyone here so far."

Harold could relate. He couldn't imagine enjoying himself at a party full of strangers. The only reason he'd agreed to go to this one was because of Taylor.

"You know people," Taylor said. He nodded toward a small group in the corner. "There are familiar faces right there."

"Yeah?" Joanne asked. "And if you can tell me the names of those familiar faces, I'll give you twenty bucks."

"I think the really tall one's name is Jordan."

"It's John," Melissa corrected.

"I was close."

"And the other two?" Joanne asked.

Taylor sighed. "I don't know. I usually see them at these things, but I don't talk to them."

"That's what I meant. The people we usually talk to haven't arrived yet."

"Who's coming?"

"I'm not exactly sure. I sent a group message. Tina and Alan will probably show up, but you know they're always fashionably late bordering on late. Cienna said she couldn't make it. James isn't coming, which means Ezra isn't either, but I think Justin, Andre, and Carmella said they'd stop by."

"James?" Harold asked. He shouldn't have been surprised to hear the name. Taylor had said he'd played with the man at an event like this before.

"He and Ezra are staying in for the night," Joanne replied. "What do you want to do first? I'm thinking drinks."

"Drinks sound good," Harold said. He could use one.

He was relieved to find both alcoholic and nonalcoholic options among the array set up on the kitchen counter. He grabbed a beer and twisted it open, taking a long swig.

"Are you okay?" Taylor asked quietly.

"I'll be fine." It wasn't the pup play putting him off. Harold had never liked parties. He preferred small gatherings or spending time with people one on one.

"If at any time you want to go, just say so."

"Are you telling me I can safe word out of the party?"

Taylor grinned. "That's not a bad idea. What's your word? Archipelago?"

"How about I just tell you I want to go home?"

"That works, but it's less fun."

Harold should have responded with a tease of some sort, but he wasn't feeling it at the moment.

Everyone got their drinks and they moved back into the living room, becoming one of the small groups taking up space there.

"We haven't been introduced," Harold said to Melissa.

"No, we haven't. I'm Melissa. And you're the hot Daddy Taylor's been living with, right?"

"Why does everyone insist on calling me that?"

"You really have to ask?" She sounded honestly curious.

"His name is Harold," Taylor interjected. "And stop

trying to make him a Daddy. He's a Master. My Master, so keep your grubby little paws off him."

My Master. The words sent a shock through Harold's body like lightning. Taylor had called him Master before, but this felt different. This wasn't just a title for playing. He was claiming Harold as his own. Harold couldn't help the stupid grin that split his face, and he tried his best to hide it behind another swig of his beer. When he felt he'd recovered enough composure, he said, "I don't know anything about being a Daddy, but being a Master suits me quite well."

The girls giggled. "You two are adorable," Melissa said. "I'm kind of jealous."

"Excuse me?" Joanne said with a tug on her leash. "You have a Mistress of your own, you know."

"Temporarily," Melissa pouted.

"Yeah, well, let's see how you do tonight, and maybe we'll discuss extending your contract."

Contracts. Now that was something Harold had never expected to talk about at a party.

The conversation turned to ordinary things, catching up with each other, how was work going, who was the latest model Taylor got to work with, etcetera. Harold was content to listen to it and contribute on occasion.

As more guests arrived, the familiar faces turned into actual acquaintances. People stopped by to say hi to Taylor, Joanne, and Melissa and chat for a few minutes before wandering to another group or downstairs. Harold was curious about the basement and the pup playroom, but if he never found out what a kink dungeon looked like, he wouldn't mind.

Tilting his bottle back, he found that it was empty. "I'm gonna get another drink," he said. "Anyone want anything?"

"Would you mind getting us some water?" Joanne asked.

"In a bottle or a bowl?"

Joanne smiled. "Two bottles will be fine. Thank you."

"Do you want me to come with you?" Taylor asked.

Harold shook his head. "I can carry two bottles of water and a beer. You hang out with your friends."

He headed toward the kitchen and grabbed the drinks plus an additional water for Taylor. He hadn't been gone more than a couple of minutes. When he returned there was a tall man in black leather pants with a harness over his chest wrapping an arm around Taylor. Anger filled Harold at the sight. *How dare he touch what's mine?* The thought made him hesitate for a second, wondering where such possessiveness had sprung from, but he pushed it aside to examine later. The stranger pawing his pup needed to be dealt with *now*.

He approached the group and handed Joanne two of the waters before turning to the man. "I thought it was rude to touch what doesn't belong to you."

The man smirked. "He doesn't look claimed to me."

"Because he's not glued to my side? I don't need a leash to bring a pup to heel."

"God, that's sexy," he heard Joanne whisper.

Before the man could utter another word, Harold ordered, "Taylor. Kneel."

It was a relief knowing Taylor had the kneepads on because he dropped to the floor so fast it was as if his legs no longer knew how to function. He crawled forward and rubbed his face against Harold's leg, whimpering.

"You did nothing wrong, pup. I'm not angry with you."

Taylor settled down and leaned against him. Harold

petted his head idly as he asked, "Does he look claimed now?"

"You should put a collar on him," the man said. "It would make things easier for other people to know he's taken."

"Taken or not, it's common courtesy to ask before touching someone. If you'd asked him, he would have told you who he belonged to. No collar necessary."

The man shrugged and moved on. Harold wasn't satisfied, but before he could argue further, Joanne and Melissa jumped in front of him, blocking his sight of the stranger's retreating back.

"Oh my god, that was so hot," Melissa said.

"Are you sure we can't convince you to be a Daddy?" Joanne asked. "Because I really want you to spank me. Like, right now."

Well, that was embarrassing. "Sorry, ladies. Even if I was interested in trying the kink, I'm only interested in men."

"Damn," Joanne said. "Foiled twice. Taylor, you are one lucky son of a bitch."

Taylor didn't respond to her. He was looking up at Harold with an urgency Harold couldn't decipher. He pressed against Harold's leg for emphasis.

"We're going to go find a big strong Dom to play with," Joanne announced. "Maybe you should take Taylor somewhere with a little privacy?"

"Where would I find that?"

"Ironically, the best place would probably be outside. The backyard is enclosed so no one can see."

Harold could use some fresh air. "Come on, boy," he said and headed toward the kitchen where he'd spotted a door to the backyard earlier.

There was a large awning covering the space behind the house, and the whole yard was fenced in. There were other people around but few enough that they could find their own semiprivate space. Harold took a seat on a folding chair, and Taylor crawled after him. Harold worried about him damaging his kneepads, but Taylor didn't seem concerned. He moved to kneel between Harold's legs and thrust his face forward into Harold's crotch.

"Whoa, what are you doing?"

Taylor nuzzled, making it clear what he was aiming for.

"What's gotten into you?"

Excitement, apparently. Taylor wriggled and if he'd had a tail, it would have been wagging. He leaned forward again, and Harold pushed him back with a hand on his shoulder.

"As much as I'd normally love this idea, I'm not having sex with you in front of an audience, pup."

Taylor sat back, but he was still restless, rubbing his face against Harold's knee.

"Last time you acted like this, you were really happy. Is that it? Are you happy I claimed you?"

Taylor barked an affirmative. Harold smiled and cupped his face. "Of course I did. You said you'd be mine here. I wasn't going to let some random guy put his hands on you."

Taylor pushed up to lick Harold's cheek. Harold laughed. "Okay, okay. I get it. You're happy. I'm happy you're happy." He pulled back to look Taylor in the face again. "I think you need to work off some of this excess energy. How about we go find the playroom?"

Taylor barked again, and Harold got up to lead him back inside. The stairs to the basement were on the other side of the living room. Harold didn't see Joanne and

Melissa as they cut through the crowd. He wondered if they'd found the Dom they were looking for.

The staircase ended in a short hall with a door on either side. To their left was the playroom. The floor was covered in thick padding. A bunch of pups were already inside, wrestling with each other, playing with balls, squeakers, and other toys. To the right was the dungeon, which looked surprisingly more ordinary than Harold had expected. The white walls and wood flooring matched the interior of the rest of the house, and although the furniture was unrecognizable, the room had an airiness to it.

The main things that lent any sense of "dungeon" to the atmosphere were a set of chains hanging from the ceiling and the thumping bass that he recognized as the sound he'd heard when they'd first walked up the driveway. The number of implements hanging on hooks along the walls or on shelves was intimidating. He recognized the paddles and floggers from his online searches, but there were other things whose function he couldn't even imagine.

Turning his back on the dungeon, he faced the playroom again. "Go on, pup."

Taylor immediately bounded into the room. The other pups were quick to welcome him, and soon he was chasing balls and wrestling with them.

The joy on Taylor's face as he played could light up a room. Even with his mask on, Harold could see the elation in his eyes. It was different than when he did this at home. Being able to share his kink with others who understood and felt the same lit him up inside. Harold realized this was a need for Taylor, just like all the other things they'd done together.

The knowledge was an epiphany. He'd always assumed Taylor went to these parties because he liked them and they gave him an opportunity to be a pup when he didn't have that at home. Perhaps that was true. He'd been having a good time hanging out with his friends, and he was certainly a part of this community, but Harold believed there was more to it than that. There was something Taylor gained from this room in particular that could not be found anywhere else. It wasn't about having a Master or an opportunity to play. It was this connection to other pups, this interaction that was innocent, boundless, and free. Harold could never give that to Taylor on his own or without bringing him to parties like this one.

Taylor had no idea how long he'd been playing for. Eventually, thirst brought his attention to things other than his fellow pups and the squeaky ball he'd been trying to bite. He looked around for Harold and didn't see him at first.

"Over here, pup."

He turned and there was his Master. He must have been watching the whole time. Taylor padded over to him and was greeted with pets to the head. He let out a happy yip.

"Having a good time? How about we get you some water?"

His Master was always so good to him. Taylor voiced his agreement, then followed Harold back upstairs where his Master got him a bowl of water. While he was drinking, Joanne and Melissa joined them.

"Find what you were looking for?" Harold asked.

"We had a very good time in the dungeon," Joanne said. "How about you two?"

"Taylor spent a couple of hours in the pup room."

A couple of hours? Had it really been that long? He'd been having such a good time, he hadn't noticed.

"We're thinking of heading home," Joanne said.

Harold looked down at him. "What do you say, pup? You want to stay longer or are you ready to leave?"

Taylor wanted to curl up on the couch at home, but he wasn't looking forward to the train ride to get there. He'd have to walk on two legs and be a person again. He wasn't ready for that.

Harold knelt down in front of him. "If you can put your clothes on and walk to the car, we can take a cab home."

When did Harold become clairvoyant?

A cab ride from Queens to home would be a hefty bill. Taylor whined.

"It's okay, pup," Harold said. "You ready to go home?"

Taylor rubbed his cheek against Harold's knee.

"We can split the cab," Joanne suggested.

"Sounds good."

Taylor spent the car ride curled against Harold's side. He remained glued there as they went up to Harold's apartment.

"Couch cuddle time?"

As if he had to ask.

"Do you want your mask?"

Taylor shook his head no. He just wanted to stay close.

His Master seemed content with that idea. He stretched out on the couch and patted the space beside him. Taylor lay down next to him, resting his head on Harold's chest. Harold turned on the TV, and they lay that way for a while.

"Thank you," Taylor said when he was feeling up to speech again.

"What for?"

"Going to the party with me. I know you didn't get to do much."

"I got to watch you."

Taylor looked up at him. "I meant you didn't get to do anything for you."

Harold cupped his cheek. "Seeing you happy is always what I want to do."

That wasn't fair. Taylor was already attached. Did Harold want him to fall completely? "You had a good time then?"

"You did, and that's what matters."

That didn't answer Taylor's question. Or maybe it did.

"It's late," Harold said. "How about we go to bed?"

Taylor nodded.

And then, with a mischievous quirk to his lips, Harold picked him up and carried him to the bedroom.

Taylor's heart swooned.

———

Monday morning was rough. In addition to lack of sleep from the party (worth it), Taylor had woken wrapped in Harold's arms and didn't want to leave them. When Harold had carried him to bed, he'd laid Taylor down like a boyfriend and not a pup. He'd kissed him and caressed him and brought him to a sweet climax before they'd drifted off to sleep together. How was he supposed to leave this cocoon of snuggly blankets and perfect Master?

He'd snoozed the alarm a full half hour before he reluctantly forced himself to rise. After brushing his teeth and putting on work clothes, he felt himself even begin to shine. The party had totally been worth the slow morning. He felt relaxed, refreshed, rejuvenated; all those R words people got after going to a spa. And during his lunch break he was going to meet his future roommate. Things were going well.

The potential roommate, Fiore, agreed to meet him at a café across the street from his office. Taylor entered and scanned the room. At a table against one wall sat a dark olive-skinned person with curly black hair and a turquoise scarf wrapped around their shoulders. Taylor approached the table.

"Fiore?"

"Taylor?"

"The scarf was a good idea. Otherwise, I'd be introducing myself to everyone in here."

Fiore leaned back and gestured for Taylor to sit. "You might have made a lot of new friends that way."

"Or pissed off a bunch of people who want to eat their lunch in peace."

"Finding out which is the fun part."

"I don't have time for that. My lunch break's only an hour."

"We should get down to business then. Why don't you go order something, and we'll discuss the possibility of being roommates."

Taylor ordered a BLT and a ginger ale and resumed his seat while he waited for the order to be ready.

"Okay," Fiore said. "I have a few things to address at the start. They're make-or-break. Best to get them out of the way first."

"Sounds reasonable," Taylor said. "What are they?"

"Neatness for one. I can't live with a slob."

"Are we talking general neatness or OCD level?"

"General neatness. Wash your own dishes after you use them, keep the bathroom clean, no clothing all over the floor."

"Fine by me. What's the second thing?"

"Rent on time. I'm not getting stuck with debt that isn't mine."

"For the past six months, I've been living with my ex because we couldn't afford to move out. I'm not the type to shunt my responsibilities on others."

"You were living with your ex for six months?"

"We broke up three months after signing a lease together."

"Oh, honey. No wonder you're desperate for a new place."

Taylor laughed. "Any more things on your list?"

"One, but it's personal." They gestured toward the counter. "Your food is ready."

Taylor rose to get his lunch. When he returned, he asked, "What's your last make-or-break condition?"

"Sex."

Taylor's eyebrows rose, and Fiore chuckled.

"It's about sex. You're welcome to have it, but I'm not interested in it, and I'd rather not hear it at all hours."

"So fuck when you're not home or do it quietly."

"Exactly. What are your make-or-break conditions?"

"I think you covered the basics, though I'd prefer to be open about the fact that I have a particular kink I like to indulge in. You don't need to worry it will be in your face, but I'm not going to hide who I am."

Fiore smiled. "That feeling's mutual."

Not wanting to forget to eat or run out of time, Taylor took a bite of his sandwich and swallowed before asking, "This is the apartment you're already living in, yeah?"

"Yes."

"How come you're in need of a roommate?"

"My current roommate is leaving me for an ashram in India."

"That's one of those places where they do yoga and meditate, right?" Taylor asked.

"Yes. She's been wanting to go for a long time and was recently laid off from her job. The opportunity seemed meant to be."

"That's really cool. For all the traveling I do, I've never been out of the country."

"What is it you do again?" Fiore asked.

"I'm an assistant photographer for a production company."

"You travel for your job?"

"All over the country," Taylor said. "What do you do?"

"I'm sorry to say I have an ordinary corporate job, but it's paying the bills until my clothing line takes off."

"You're a fashion designer?"

"That is the dream."

"Can I see what you've designed?"

"Of course. I have an Etsy shop called Alohera. You can see my latest work there." Fiore winked. "Feel free to go shopping."

Taylor laughed. "I will."

Taylor returned to his office in a good mood. He liked Fiore. He had no idea how that opinion would hold up in the enclosed space of an apartment, but they were off to a good start. They'd agreed to meet again when they had more time to get to know each other before making any decisions.

He settled back at his desk, ready to continue the work-day. He'd barely brushed his keyboard before Meisha called out, "There you are! Pack your bags. We have a shoot in Vermont tomorrow. We leave at eight."

"What? Why such short notice?"

"The photographer who did the previous shoot for the project hasn't delivered and the deadline is Friday."

"Fuck."

"Yeah."

What could he say? His livelihood depended on work. "Meeting here or at the airport?"

"LaGuardia. I'll text you the flight details as soon as I have them."

"Do you know how long we'll be gone for?"

"Shouldn't be long. I think we'll be back Wednesday night."

After which he'd have one evening to move the furniture out of his apartment and make sure it looked decent enough for his landlord. Yeah, he could do that. Not.

"Thanks for letting me know."

"No prob."

When he was alone again, Taylor rubbed a hand over his face. How the fuck was he going to move all his furniture Thursday night? He still had to find a storage space, rent a truck, movers... His thoughts threatened to spiral. He picked up the phone and barely looked as he dialed from memory.

"Taylor? Shouldn't you be working right now?"

The sound of his Master's voice soothed the sharpest edges of Taylor's anxiety. "I was just told I have to leave tomorrow morning for a photo shoot. I'll be away for the next two days."

There was a pause, then Harold asked, "Are you worried about moving your furniture?"

Harold knew him so well. "There's so much to do, and

I'll only have one night to do it in. I don't even know where to begin."

"How about I take it off your mind?"

"This isn't going to be solved with a bath, Harold."

"I'm going to forgive the attitude since I know you're stressed," Harold said. "I wasn't talking about a scene. How do you feel about leaving me the keys to your place and while you're away, I move your furniture into a storage unit?"

The crushing pressure poised to lift from Taylor's shoulders. "You'd do that?"

"Of course, pup. I don't like to see you stressed."

The weight lifted away, and Taylor found he could breathe again. "I wish I was home so I could hug you right now."

"You can hug me all you want when you get here."

"I will." And more. He wanted to rub his face all over Harold in gratitude.

"You're welcome, pup," Harold said. "By the way, did you get a chance to meet Fiore before this news was dropped in your lap?"

"Yes! They were wonderful. We're going to meet again for more than an hour next time."

"Great," Harold said. "You can tell me all about that when you get home too."

Harold had spent the rest of Monday focused on Taylor and Tuesday finishing up some work. It wasn't until Wednesday that he had time to move Taylor's furniture, but that morning he'd woken feeling wrecked and in no mood to do so.

Was it wrong that a part of him wanted to procrastinate to keep Taylor with him longer?

It didn't help that he'd slept terribly Tuesday night, having gotten used to Taylor's presence in his bed, whether at the foot of the mattress or beside him. If one night without his pup had been torture, how was he supposed to handle sleeping alone after Taylor moved out? And he couldn't blame the feeling on habit. Even during the day, the apartment felt empty, which was ridiculous since Taylor was usually at work during those hours.

Eventually, he dragged himself out of bed and called Kossi.

"Mind doubling up on that lobster dinner? I need to empty the rest of that apartment today."

"Sorry, man. I'm fully booked. I am looking forward to cashing in on what you already owe me."

"Soon. We'll schedule something soon."

He had no idea who else he could call. His other friends either had nine-to-five jobs or were too far away to help. He'd have to get some professionals to assist him. Unless...

He called James. It was worth a try.

"You wouldn't happen to know anyone who'd be free right now to help move some furniture, would you?"

"As a matter of fact, I do know someone with time on his hands. Let me give him a call, and I'll get back to you."

"That'd be great. Thanks."

Half an hour later Harold headed out to pick up the moving truck he'd rented. He was to meet James's friend Damian at Taylor's apartment.

As soon as the man arrived, Harold knew they'd have no problem moving Taylor's things. He was half a head taller than him and built like he'd never stepped foot outside a gym.

"Harold, right? James told me you could use a hand."

"Yeah. Thanks for coming."

"No problem. James knows I'm always looking for something to occupy myself with."

"How do you two know each other?" Harold asked.

"We used to work together. We became friends while working in the field."

"What sort of work do you do?"

"Freelance. Nothing too interesting."

That was almost the same exact answer James had given him. Harold had a feeling whatever Damian did and James used to do was a lot more interesting than they let on.

"Come on. Let's get this stuff moved for your boy."

"James told you?"

"I've never met Taylor, but James has told me about him."

Harold wondered how much James had shared. "Maybe we can take you out to dinner when he gets back. As a thank you for your help."

Damian waved a hand. "No need. Like I said, I could use the distraction."

"Then let's get started."

They worked efficiently together and were able to move everything in one shot. Harold offered once more to repay Damian for his help, but he refused. They parted ways, and Harold returned to his empty apartment. Lonely, he pulled out his phone and checked his messages. There was one from Taylor.

Taylor: They've delayed our return. We won't be back until tomorrow.

Taylor: Did everything go okay with the move?

Harold felt bad for not paying attention to his messages sooner. Taylor was probably stressed about the furniture and coming home a day later than planned. He picked up the phone and dialed.

"Taylor?" he asked when the line clicked.

"Harold." Harold could hear the relief in Taylor's voice. "How did things go today?"

"Everything's in the storage unit. There's nothing to worry about."

"Did you get my text message?"

"Yes. Do you want me to pick you up from the airport?"

"I'd love that, believe me, but I have to go directly to the office after landing. We'll probably carpool there."

Harold tried to quell his disappointment. He wanted to see his pup, hold him. "I'll see you after work then."

"I want to stop by the apartment to make sure everything is clean before I have to drop off the keys on Friday. I don't know what time I'll be home."

"That's fine. You'll get here when you get here."

"Will there be a bath waiting for me?" Taylor teased.

"I don't have the patience for a bath, pup. I want to hold you."

He heard a sharp intake of breath.

"I miss you," Harold said.

"I miss you too," Taylor replied, his voice a whisper.

"Tomorrow night, pup. We'll see each other then."

One day was a short span of time, and yet it loomed before him like an eternity.

Chapter Fourteen

Taylor hung up the phone feeling much better than he had all day. He'd been worried about the move, and when Harold hadn't replied to his message, it'd given his anxiety an excuse to plague him. He'd done his best to distract himself with work, but he'd also flooded Joanne's phone with texts. She deserved an update before he went to sleep.

Taylor: Harold just called. Everything's fine and furniture's been moved.

Joanne: Told you it would be. Are you still on the phone with him?

Taylor: No. I have to wake up at the ass crack of dawn tomorrow.

Joanne: I'm surprised you're not chatting it up anyway.

Taylor: If I kept him on the phone I wouldn't hang up until sunrise.

Joanne: And this would be a problem because...?

Taylor: I have to function at work tomorrow.

Joanne: And yet you're still replying to my messages.

Taylor: It's rude to cut off a conversation.
Joanne: Sweetie, our conversations never end. It's not like you haven't fallen asleep and replied to me in the morning before.

After a pause she added,

Joanne: What's on your mind?

Taylor took his time answering, erasing part of the message three times before sending it.

Taylor: He's really good to me, you know? Like this whole thing with the move. He stepped in and helped organize everything. He volunteered his friend to help and didn't say anything about my procrastinating and the fact that it's all my fault. He just...takes care of me.

He paused for a while to see if Joanne would interject, but she was probably waiting on him to continue because they both knew his word vomit wasn't finished.

Taylor: It's not going to be the same if I move out. I know it won't.
Taylor: Even if he wants to continue seeing me and scening together, it won't be the same.
Taylor: I—

He cut the last message off before he could send it as the words rang in his head.
I don't want to leave. I want to be with him always.
I want to be his.

The phone rang.

"I hate waiting for messages. We're doing this verbally," Joanne said after he picked up.

Taylor let out a shaky breath. "I don't want to lose him, Joanne. He's my Master."

"What makes you think you're going to lose him?"

"I don't think he liked the party the other day." Something had been off in the way Harold had said he'd enjoyed watching Taylor. The reply had felt more like avoidance than the truth.

Had Harold not liked him playing with other pups? No, he hadn't lied about that. Maybe it was the Dom who'd tried to play with him? Was he regretting claiming Taylor as his own? He hoped not. Taylor knew it'd only been for the party, but he wanted Harold to do that for real.

"He didn't seem to be having a terrible time when I saw him," Joanne said. "He was quiet when we were all talking, but I figured that was because most of the people there were strangers to him."

"I thought that too, but maybe he doesn't like parties at all."

"You don't need a party to play."

No, they didn't, but Taylor's mind had gotten stuck on thinking they did. After Taylor moved out, where else could they play? Taylor would have a roommate. Even if Fiore hadn't explicitly said they didn't want to hear about Taylor's sex life, Taylor wouldn't feel comfortable letting go when someone who wasn't involved was around. The only other option was Harold's place, and although it seemed like the best option, it was the one Taylor wanted to avoid. Harold's apartment felt like home. What would it feel like going there when he was only a guest?

"There's really no reason to dwell on this now," Joanne said. "It's not like you're moving out yet."

"I might be next month."

"What?" Joanne asked, surprised.

"Shit, I forgot I hadn't told you. Remember that person who had a room for rent as of June? They called back and said it was still available. I met with them on Monday."

"Oh?"

"Yeah. They're great. A little stubborn on things, but not in any unreasonable way. I think we might be able to work as roommates."

"That's great," Joanne said. She didn't sound as enthused as the words would imply.

"Why aren't you happy for me?"

"I am happy for you."

"No, you're not. You're lying."

She sighed. "I'll be happy for you if this is what's going to make you happy."

"And why wouldn't it?"

"Because I think you'd be happier staying with Harold."

Of course he'd be happier staying with Harold, but they'd spoken about why that wasn't happening.

"Have you considered my suggestion to hint to him that you want to stay?"

"Joanne, I wouldn't even know how to go about doing that."

"Try."

"Why is it so important to you?"

"Because once you sign a lease, it's going to be too late."

The words surfed across the phone line in a rush and hit Taylor with the force of a tsunami. Once he had an apartment, it wouldn't matter if Harold asked him to stay. He'd be stuck like he'd been with Liam until the lease was over. He didn't want to go through that again.

"I know it isn't in you to impose, but if you can't ask to move in permanently, at least start a conversation about continuing your relationship after you move. Open the door, Taylor."

He had to do more than that. It wasn't just the dating and the scenes. He needed to tell Harold he wanted him as his Master, always.

Taylor groaned. "When am I going to do this? I have to work all day tomorrow, and then I need to swing by the apartment to make sure it's clean enough to get my security deposit back. Friday, I need to drop off my keys." He rubbed a hand over his face. "The weekend. It can wait for the weekend, right? This shouldn't be a rushed conversation anyway."

"You mean you want time to get it on if and when he says yes," Joanne said.

"No," Taylor objected, although feebly. He rallied a sense of righteousness and pushed on. "I meant that a conversation like this means something. It should be special in some way. It should—" He cut off as an idea came to him. "Oh my god, Joanne. I've got it!"

"What?" she asked, for once not following his scattered train of thought.

Asking Harold to be his Master was a big moment. It needed to be special, and he needed to do something special for it. "Let me think for a bit and I'll get back to you. I'll probably need your help with this."

"Okay..." she said. "Maybe you should go to sleep now. Like you said, you have to get up early, and I think you need to sleep on whatever idea's gotten into your brain before you put it into action."

"Ye of little faith."

"I will have plenty of faith after you've slept. I'll talk to you tomorrow?"

"Yeah."

He snuggled under the covers after they hung up, but he was wide awake, fleshing out his idea. Excitement thrummed through him, turning his longing to see Harold into anticipation of Harold's expression when he saw what Taylor planned to do.

I need to make this perfect. I have to get every detail just right.

Actually, there wasn't much to plan. He could see the moment in his mind's eye. The hardest part would be finding the box. He already knew what it would say.

Harold had received a text from Taylor as soon as he'd landed. Subsequent messages relayed the rate at which he acquired his luggage—slowly—and arrived at the office— even more slowly. Although he was glad his pup had returned safely, each message was a reminder that there was still a full day to wait before he could hold Taylor in his arms. He tried to lose himself in the world of computer programming, but his mind refused to focus. Eventually, he gave up and called James.

"I thought the furniture had all been moved," James said in lieu of a hello.

"It has and thank you again for calling Damian."

"Anytime. The man is often desperate for distraction."

"So he said."

"To what do I owe the pleasure of this phone call if you aren't in need of assistance?"

"Are you free for lunch? I'm the one in need of distraction right now."

"Taylor isn't home yet?"

"He'll be home tonight."

"Ah. How does Martini's on Fifth sound?"

"I can be there in twenty."

James was already seated at a table by the window when Harold arrived. "Hope you don't mind that I keep calling out of the blue like this," Harold said as he slid into the chair across from him.

"Not at all. I could use more friends in the city. Most of my acquaintances are related to my old job. It's...not always comfortable seeing them."

"What about Damian?"

"Damian is an exception."

"I could also use more friends in the city. I'm not the best at going out and meeting people."

"Prefer to be behind a screen?"

"It is one of the places I'm most comfortable," Harold admitted.

"There's always social media."

Harold shuddered and James laughed. "I'll take that as a no."

"It's fine for keeping in touch, but I don't understand the concept of building friendships with people you've never met. How do you interpret someone's tone and meaning when you can't see their face? And don't tell me video chat is a thing. It's not the same."

"I agree with you. I'm not one for InstaFaceTweeting either. I only suggested it because I know you like computers."

"InstaFaceTweeting." Harold laughed. "Computers and the internet are two different things. The internet and social media are two different things. Social media is a beast all on its own."

"More like an offspring."

"An unsupervised teenage offspring," Harold agreed.

James lifted his water glass for a toast. "To meeting friends in person, then."

Harold clinked the glass with his own and took a sip. "Ugh, I need a beer. This is not going to cut it."

James waved to get the server's attention. "Two beers coming up. Have we decided what we want to order yet?"

"Burgers. Fries. With bacon and extra grease."

"So much for being the adult generation," James said.

"Being an adult means realizing it's your choice whether you make bad decisions or not. And acknowledging that sometimes it's okay to have ice cream for breakfast."

"I haven't done ice cream for breakfast," James said, "but I am adding fried pickles to our menu choices. They have them as an appetizer here."

"You don't have to go with my greasy meal plan. Feel free to order something else."

"As you said, I'm an adult, and it's my choice. Today I'm having the bacon burger and I'm even adding extra cheese."

"Rebel."

James winked. "Absolutely."

Once their orders were sorted and drinks delivered, James swirled his bottle and asked, "How's Taylor?"

"Stressed. He flew back this morning from a photo shoot, and his lease is up tomorrow."

"What's his plan?"

"He's staying with me for now, but he's been talking to someone who may have a room for him in June."

"And you're okay with him leaving?"

"No." The word burst out of him, raw and unstoppable.

"Then why is he leaving?" James asked.

Harold let out a frustrated sigh. "Because I haven't asked him to stay yet. Every time I want to, something interrupts me."

"Is that the only reason?"

Harold took a deep breath, let it out slowly, and shook his head. "A part of me is wondering if I should."

"Why?" James sounded surprised. Harold couldn't blame him. Up until Sunday he'd had no reason to doubt his desire to ask Taylor to stay, but his concern had always been about giving Taylor what he needed. After the party, he wasn't fully sure he could.

He hadn't planned to talk about this when he'd called James, but who else could he discuss these things with? "We went to a party on Sunday. I think you knew about it?"

James nodded.

"I'm not really a fan of parties in general, so I wasn't... enthused about going to this one."

"Not wanting to go to a party isn't a make-or-break deal for most relationships," James said.

"The party wasn't as bad as I'd anticipated," Harold admitted. "What surprised me was seeing what Taylor got out of it."

"From what I've seen in the past, Taylor uses public events as opportunities to scene," James said. "He doesn't need to do that if you're his Master."

"It's not the scenes. It's the community and the opportunity to play with other pups like him."

James gestured between the two of them. "You have community right here. Taylor too."

Harold wasn't saying this right. He ran a hand through his hair. "I can't get it out of my head how happy he was playing with those other pups. There was a freedom to it that had nothing to do with serving a Master."

"Harold." James waited until Harold looked at him before continuing. "It's impossible for you to be everything Taylor needs, and you can't expect to provide it all by yourself. That's what community is for. And community doesn't have to come in the form of a house party. Any time you want to make a play date, Ezra would be happy to spend time with Taylor."

Harold had followed James's words right up until the end. "What?"

"Ezra. Pup play isn't his main kink, but he loves indulging in it. Having a place to do that and someone he knows to do it with would be a boon. I would appreciate it as well. Like you, I don't care for parties, and I would prefer he play with someone we both know instead of random acquaintances."

Why hadn't Harold thought of that? All of James's reasons echoed his own, and he was sure Taylor would love playing with Ezra. He smiled. "That would be fantastic."

"There you go," James said with a sweep of his arm. "Problem solved. Now you can ask him to move in permanently."

Harold laughed. "I think I'll give him until the weekend to get things sorted first."

James shrugged. "Suit yourself. Right now, it's time for fried pickles."

Taylor couldn't wait to get home. He ached for a comfy place to lie down, blankets, good food, and, above all, Harold, but first he had to check on his apartment. He was too paranoid not to see it one more time before he left for good. He'd just turned onto his street when he saw his Master standing in front of his building.

"What are you doing here?" Taylor asked.

"I thought I'd surprise you. Hope you don't mind."

Was he kidding? It was all Taylor could do to keep from launching himself into Harold's arms. He shook his head, his smile uncontrollably wide. "I'm glad you came."

Perhaps it should have been a momentous moment, but Taylor felt nothing as he walked the perimeter of his apartment. His connection to the place had been severed long before his things had been removed.

When they stepped back outside, Harold asked, "Have you eaten?"

"Not yet."

"We'll pick up something on the way." He gestured toward Taylor's duffel bag. "Let me carry that."

"Are you sure?" Taylor asked, even as he handed it over. They turned in the direction of the subway and started walking.

"You said everything went okay with the furniture?" Taylor asked.

Harold nodded. "It's all in the storage unit, and we have that for a month."

"Let me know what I owe you for the movers and stuff."

Harold waved it off. "Don't worry about it."

"Harold, I can't let you pay for it. It's my responsibility."

"We can discuss it later. How about we get you home first?"

Home. The word tugged at Taylor's heart like a lure. "Okay."

Harold slung an arm over his shoulders and pulled him closer. The warmth and familiarity of him soaked into

Taylor like a balm. Exhaustion overtook him as the stresses of the past few days loosened their grip.

"Harold? Can we just crash tonight?"

"We can do whatever you want, pup. As long as you sleep next to me, I don't care what we do."

Yes. He wanted to sleep just like this tonight.

They moved directly to the couch as soon as they got home. Taylor had barely enough time to put the bag of takeout on the coffee table before Harold toppled him onto the cushions.

"I thought we were eating dinner," Taylor said.

"Are you hungry?" Harold asked.

"Not really." Taylor snuggled closer and rested his head on Harold's shoulder. Harold kissed the top of his head, and he tilted his face up for one on his lips. Harold obliged. "Another, please," Taylor said, and Harold did it again. "Another," Taylor repeated softly.

This time Harold lingered. They shifted so Taylor lay back on the couch and Harold could lean on top of him. Taylor's arms were free to wrap around Harold, and he pulled the man closer as they kissed.

"Harold," Taylor whispered. "Take me to bed. Please."

Harold maneuvered half off the couch so he could stand up without breaking their embrace. He carried Taylor into the bedroom and laid him down gently. Their kissing resumed, this time with hands reaching beneath clothing.

"Harold," Taylor called again. "I want you inside me."

"Yes." The word emerged as if ripped from the depths of Harold's soul. Need and hunger followed on its heels, turning their touches from soft, tickling caresses to purposeful movements and clutching grasps. It was as if they could meld together if they pulled each other close enough.

"Skin," Taylor said as he panted, and Harold nodded. He opened Taylor's pants and shifted down the bed, pulling them with him until Taylor's legs were free and bare. He lifted one of Taylor's feet, mouthing the instep and working his way up to the ankle.

"Harold." Taylor gasped.

The man continued to worship Taylor's leg from ankle to knee, knee to thigh, and finally from thigh to groin.

"Harold!" Taylor cried when Harold's teeth nipped the delicate flesh between his legs.

"Take your shirt off," Harold ordered, and Taylor scrambled to obey. They fumbled together until Taylor was fully naked and splayed like a starfish.

"You too," Taylor said.

Harold was quick to dispose of his own clothing, but the wait still felt like an eternity. Taylor eagerly welcomed him back into his arms, desperate to feel the touch of skin against skin for the full length of his body. It was perfect.

"Like this," he said. "Just like this."

"Yes."

Harold reached for the bedside drawer to grab supplies. He worked blindly to open the lube bottle as they kissed again. Taylor felt him reach between them and down to circle a finger around Taylor's hole. Given their urgency, Taylor expected him to make quick work of foreplay, but he didn't. Instead, he teased, he pressed, and he meandered lazily. His kisses matched the pace of his fingers, nipping and biting, sucking, or pecking with no rhyme or reason.

"What are you doing?" Taylor asked while Harold nibbled his jaw.

"I'm enjoying the feel of your skin against mine and having you beneath me."

"Oh."

Harold slipped a finger fully inside Taylor, wiggled it in a circle as if to measure if there was enough room, then removed it and replaced it with two. The change was sudden and tight and made Taylor cry out.

"You wanted me in you," Harold said.

"This wasn't what I meant."

"I know, but now that I have you back, I don't want to let go too quickly."

A lump lodged itself in Taylor's throat. "Don't." He cleared it. "Don't, then. Take all the time you want."

Harold smiled wickedly. "Are you sure?" he asked. "I fully plan to indulge myself."

Taylor nodded. "Please. I want to be with you."

"All right."

Harold had worked Taylor open further while they spoke and now he slipped a third digit in. Taylor felt Harold's fingers undulate, massaging his insides and brushing his prostate.

"A little..." Taylor said as he squirmed.

"Want something, pup?"

"You have to..." Taylor shifted again but no matter how hard he tried, he couldn't get Harold's fingers where he wanted them to go. He blew out a breath. "You're doing this on purpose."

Harold grinned. "You said you didn't mind if I indulged myself."

"You're just going to tease me?"

"No. In fact, I'd like you to sit up for me." Harold pushed up and back, moving much farther away than Taylor would like, though at the moment, any distance was too much. Taylor sat up and moved to follow him, wanting to close the gap. "That's it, pup. Come here."

Harold arranged them so he was sitting on the mattress

with Taylor straddling his lap. Taylor approved of the position since it gave him the opportunity to wrap his arms around Harold and press their bodies close.

"You going to move for me?" Harold asked as he slipped his fingers back inside Taylor. They squelched, and Taylor realized he'd added more lube to them, much more than necessary.

"If you want."

"I do want." Taylor could feel Harold's fingers curve and they pressed tauntingly against his prostate. "If you want as well, you'll have to move."

Oh. *He wants me to work for it.* Taylor rose, letting Harold's fingers slide out a little and then sank back down. Harold pressed firmly enough that when his fingers reached that sweet spot, it had the effect Taylor was looking for. His lips parted on a groan.

"Like that?" Harold asked.

Taylor nodded.

"Want some more?"

Taylor nodded again and began working himself up and down on Harold's hand. The excess lube made vulgar sounds with each thrust.

"I didn't know you like things sounding so dirty," Taylor said.

"Sometimes it's fun," Harold replied.

As long as Taylor kept moving, Harold's touch remained relentless in bringing him pleasure. He began to sweat, clinging to the older man as his legs began to shake.

"Harold, I can't..."

"Keep going, pup. You haven't fallen apart yet."

"I don't want to come like this."

"You're still a long way off from coming."

"But..." With each movement, his cock slid along

Harold's stomach. He shifted his hips closer to gain more stimulation.

"Keep going, baby," Harold said. "Just a little more, okay?"

Taylor nodded and continued.

***

If Harold entered Taylor right now, he'd burst in three seconds. He was so eager to be inside his pup he knew he wouldn't last, and he couldn't let their first time be over so quickly.

"Do you want me to help you?" he asked when Taylor flagged again.

Taylor nodded, and Harold maneuvered his boy to give himself better leverage. He began working his fingers in short, fast movements directly on Taylor's prostate. By now he knew exactly where it was. Taylor cried out and scrabbled his hands over Harold's back. The wet sounds of the lubricant were lost to Taylor's cries as Harold continued. He didn't let up until Taylor shouted his name, the warning clear in his voice.

Taylor was trembling as Harold eased him back down on his lap, then gently maneuvered him to lie on the mattress. As if a switch had been flipped, his desire to push turned into a need to care and comfort. He brushed away the strands of hair stuck to Taylor's face from sweat and soothed him as he donned a condom and settled between his pup's legs.

"Are you all right?" he asked softly.

Taylor nodded. "Please."

Harold entered him, easing in until he could move no farther. Taylor wrapped his arms around him, bringing them back to the position in which they had started. *I belong here.* They fit together like the proper key for a lock, and Harold never wanted to break away.

"Just like this," he whispered.

Taylor smiled. "Yes. Just like this."

Harold kissed him as he rocked his hips, the pace a counterpoint to the frantic stimulation he'd given Taylor earlier. Taylor matched his rhythm, and together they rode the wave to bliss.

As he'd expected, Harold crested first, but Taylor was not long after, and as his pup floated on the afterglow, Harold heard him murmur, "Thank you, Master," followed by the barest whisper of the word "Home."

Home. The term had never been more pertinent. He'd lived in this apartment for years, but it'd been a long time since it had felt so much like home, and that was all because of Taylor.

Chapter Fifteen

Taylor woke the next morning still wrapped in Harold's arms.

This is how I want to wake up every morning.

He remembered the feelings he'd had as he'd drifted off to sleep, sated with an orgasm and exhausted from good things instead of the stresses that had plagued him all week.

He snuggled closer, expecting to feel stickiness as he wiggled, but he felt nothing of the sort. Taylor blinked his eyes open in surprise.

He cleaned me up before going to sleep!

Gently, he lifted the blanket and looked down at his body. Yes, he was clean. No sign of dried cum or even the stink of sweat. Taylor bit his lip as his eyes burned.

This man treats me so well. It's too much, how well he takes care of me.

There was no way he could leave. He had to find a way to stay here. He couldn't imagine living anywhere else.

No, it's not the apartment. It's Harold I can't be without. Harold is my home.

He needed to talk to Harold like Joanne had said. He

had to at least start the conversation, and he needed to do it *now*.

The sound of his alarm informed him that "now" would have to be "after work." If he lingered any longer, he'd be late.

But the thought kept returning to him throughout the day and when he went to return his keys to his landlord.

I can't just blurt it out to him. I'd be too worked up. And I need to make it something special. I want him to know how much he means to me.

He remembered the idea he'd come up with and called Joanne.

"Hey you, what's up?" she asked.

"Could you give me a hand with something?"

"Would this have anything to do with that idea you had the other day?"

"Yup."

"I'm listening."

The explanation was short in comparison to the epic feeling the idea gave him. That was what he wanted the moment to be. Epic, like something from a movie. Maybe he'd been influenced by the romcoms he'd made Harold watch recently on Netflix, but why couldn't life be like a movie sometimes?

"What do you think?" he asked when he was finished.

"I think it's adorably romantic, and if the man doesn't scoop you up and keep you forever, I may have to kill him."

"So, you'll help me?"

"Of course," she said. "There's only one hitch."

"What?" Chills skittered across his back as he imagined his whole plan crumbling before him.

"How are you going to get Harold out of the apartment?"

"Oh." *Good question.* "Maybe I can get James to call him?"

"Has he been to the gym lately?"

"I don't know, but since I've been away a couple of days, he might not want to go."

"You figure out how to get Harold out of the apartment, and I'll get the props ready."

"Thanks, Joanne."

"Of course. That's what best friends are for."

It had all seemed like a good idea until the moment Taylor was crouched in a cardboard box in the middle of Harold's living room, clad only in his pup gear and a G-string, waiting for Harold to return from picking up dessert.

Getting food had been the best idea he could come up with to get Harold out of the apartment. That had proven harder than he'd anticipated because everywhere delivered dinner whether it was directly or through a service. Thankfully, that wasn't the case with some dessert places.

Coordinating the timing with Joanne had been a circus. They'd set a general time for her to be in the area, but he couldn't let her wait too long. She'd look like a weirdo hanging around outside the apartment building with a huge box and duct tape. As soon as Harold had exited the front door, he'd called her, messaged the front desk to tell them she should be let in, unlocked the door, scrambled to change his clothes, and made the sign. While he did that, she'd waited for Harold to leave and then maneuvered the box into the elevator and up to the apartment. They'd thrown everything together in a hurry, and she'd left while he was still trying to catch his breath, his heart racing from the rush and growing anticipation.

Alone, that anticipation had turned into anxiety. When he'd come up with the idea, he'd pictured everything to the last detail. He'd thought it would be a grand romantic gesture. Now he felt like an idiot. How was this the way to start a conversation? He was going to completely embarrass himself.

Sweat prickled all along his back. He had to get out. If he could get out, change, and hide the evidence, Harold would never know. But Harold would be home any minute. If Taylor had any chance of pretending this had never happened, he needed to move *now*.

He lifted his leg to climb out, but the box was waist high. He'd needed Joanne's help and a chair to get into it in the first place. He wasn't going to be able to get out without tipping it over.

"Shit."

He tried again, lifting his foot over the edge and positioning it so he'd hopefully catch himself instead of collapsing to the floor when he leaned forward. He'd just braced himself to tilt the box and go for it when he heard a key in the lock. Harold was home.

"Oh fuck," he said. Then the door swung open.

***

Harold had decided to talk to Taylor over dessert. All the things Taylor had had to do over the week were done and now nothing stood before them but the weekend. Harold wanted Taylor to enjoy it, not spend it frantically working out moving logistics and housing. He didn't want Taylor thinking about housing at all, so as he returned from picking up the pastries and bubble tea Taylor had requested for dessert, he told himself tonight was the night. No more interruptions. He was going to actually start this conversation for once and finish it.

He'd just opened the door to the apartment when the words *Taylor, I'd like to talk to you about something* froze on his tongue. In the middle of his living room was a gigantic cardboard box. Taylor was inside it, dressed like he'd been the day they'd met on the sidewalk, except instead of being groggy with a hangover, he was currently standing with one leg up like a dog about to pee. Harold only had a moment to notice the handwritten sign on the side of the box that said, "Won't you be my Master?" before the whole thing fell over and Taylor windmilled to the ground.

"Taylor!" Harold rushed to his pup's side. "Are you all right?"

"No, I'm not all right," Taylor complained. "I can't believe you saw me like that." His cheeks were red with embarrassment.

Harold cupped his face, feeling the warmth of Taylor's blush against his palm. "I meant, are you hurt?"

"Only my pride."

"It'll heal." Harold helped his pup to stand. "Dare I ask what this is all about?"

Taylor gestured to the box. "It was supposed to be romantic."

Harold bit his lip. The idea might have been romantic, but what he'd seen had been more comedy than romance. As he righted the box and saw the sign's message, his humor faded. "Are you serious, pup? You want me to be your Master?"

Taylor nodded. "I want to belong to you. I've wanted to for a long time."

Harold felt light-headed. "I've wanted that too," he said.

Taylor looked at him, his eyes wide. "Really?"

"Yes. I like taking care of you, giving you what you need, making you happy. I can't imagine not having you with me every day. This week was…"

"Torture," Taylor finished for him. "It wasn't just the move stressing me out. I…I don't want to move at all."

Harold caressed his cheek. "Why didn't you say anything?"

Taylor caught his hand with his own and nuzzled. "Because this is your place, and I don't like to impose."

"Oh, pup." Harold pulled him close and hugged him. "I'm sorry I didn't ask you sooner. I've been trying to get the question out for days now."

"You have?"

"Yes, but something always got in the way." He pulled back to look Taylor in the eye. "I'd even made a point to ask you tonight but then I came home to…" He looked pointedly at the box. Taylor's face reddened again. "Since I have your attention now, before anything interrupts me, I want to ask you—will you move in with me?"

The glowing smile and excited "Yes!" Harold expected was not forthcoming. Instead, Taylor's brow furrowed and he said, "My foot's wet."

"What?"

"Oh shit! The drinks!"

"Shit!" Harold exclaimed.

They separated and looked down. In Harold's haste to check on Taylor, he'd totally forgotten the bag of pastries and tea he'd been holding. Most of it looked intact, but one of the tall cups had fallen over, disconnecting its cover and allowing the contents to spread across the floor.

"Get some paper towels. Quick!" Harold ordered as he

stooped to right the cup. Taylor scampered off to do as bid and returned in moments with a bundle of paper towels in his hands. Together they mopped up the mess.

"Aw," Taylor complained. "It got on the pastry box, and it's all soggy."

"Let's get a plate and see what we can salvage."

They managed to save everything but the puff pastry, which had become too saturated. They moved the survivors to the coffee table and settled down on the couch once they were done cleaning up.

"I'm getting the feeling romantic may be beyond us," Harold said.

"I wouldn't say that. You were doing really well before we noticed the bubble tea."

"You never answered my question."

Taylor snuggled in closer. "Yes, I would love to move in with you."

Harold put an arm around him and kissed the top of his head. "Good."

"You know, you never answered my question."

"Which question was that?"

Taylor pointed to the box. It'd been moved against the wall during their cleanup, and they could easily see the handwritten sign asking, "Won't you be my Master?"

Harold thought then of the delayed plane ride where he'd first met Taylor, the chance encounter in a cardboard box, and all the circumstances that had led them to this moment. The universe truly worked in mysterious ways to bring people together. He couldn't be more grateful for the gift.

He smiled and hugged Taylor tighter. "Yes, pup. I would love to be your Master."

Share the Love

If you enjoyed this story (or even if you didn't), please consider leaving a review on the site where you purchased it or on Goodreads.

Acknowledgments

First, I want to say thank you to my beta readers, Katie, Puck, Jill, and Anya. You were a massive help in improving this book from the skeleton it started as, and for pointing out that people can't make cell phone calls without a cell phone. >_< Lots of love to my editor, Jenni Lea. Your input is always invaluable, for both the good sentences and the ones that need work. Thank you to Jennifer, for putting up with all my questions, especially when they were repetitive. An immense thank you to Xier, for the beautiful illustrations of Taylor and Harold. I'm so glad I got to work with you, and I hope to do so again one day in the future. And to Kanaxa for making what began as an idea into my head into a stunning cover.

Last but definitely not least, thank you to you, the person who bought this book. My readers mean the world to me.

Also By Jacqueline Grey

Ghost House

Piotr and the Beast

Suit of Harte's Series

Tricks and Bids

Shoot the Moon

Limits and Stakes

Suit of Harte's Omnibus (print only)

About the Author

Jacqueline Grey lives on an island on the east coast of the United States. She spends her time juggling her day job along with her many interests, which include reading, writing, being a cat couch, and drinking tea. Sometimes she does more than one at the same time. She loves M/M romance and looks forward to bringing more stories of love into the world in the future.

You can find Jacqueline on Twitter, in her Facebook group Tea, Books, and Cats, or you can email her at JacquelineGreyBooks@gmail.com.

For simple updates on Jacqueline's books and events, check out her Facebook page or visit her website www. JacquelineGrey.com and sign up for her newsletter.

www.ingramcontent.com/pod-product-compliance
Lightning Source LLC
Chambersburg PA
CBHW021316190726
48288CB00003B/857